The Guardian

Nancy Rue

PUBLISHING

Colorado Springs, Colorado

Library of Congress Cataloging-in-Publication Data
Rue, Nancy N.
      The guardian / Nancy Rue.
            p. cm.—(Christian heritage series: 3)
      Summary: In colonial Massachusetts in 1690, Josiah, Hope, and their cousin Rebecca
overcome their differences and restore their friendship to form a "merry band."
      ISBN 1-56179-348-5
      [1. Puritans—Fiction.   2. Massachusetts—History—Colonial period, ca. 1600-1775—
Fiction.   3. Cousins—Fiction.   4. Christian life—Fiction.]   I. Title.   II. Series: Rue,
Nancy N. Christian heritage series: 3.
PZ7.R88515Gu   1995
[Fic]—dc20   94-41919
                                                                                                      CIP

                                                                                                        AC

Published by Focus on the Family Publishing,
Colorado Springs, Colorado 80995.
Distributed by Word Books, Dallas, Texas.

Editor: Gloria Kempton
Cover Design: Bradley Lind
Cover Illustration: Jeff Haynie

Printed in the United States of America

95 96 97 98 99/10 9 8 7 6 5 4 3 2 1

For Laura Danley,
who loves and understands the little Rebeccas of the world

Chapter One

"Hope! Hope, did you hear that?"

Hope Hutchinson poked a tousled head of black curls out of her bed curtain and glared at her brother, Josiah, with dark, sleep-swollen eyes. "What?"

"Did you hear that?" Josiah asked again.

"No, I didn't hear it! I'm half deaf—yes, even in my sleep." She shot him one more withering look and started to flop down on her bed cushions again.

"I heard the wolves!" Josiah said.

"You dreamed you heard them. Go back to sleep."

"No—I heard them howling! I did!"

There was no answer from behind the bed curtains. It would take more than her 11-year-old brother crying wolf to pull a 13-year-old girl out from under her eiderdown quilt on an autumn Massachusetts night.

Josiah knew that, but he said "I *heard* them!" once more

before crawling out of his cot and creeping across the cold plank floor to the window. He leaned against the pane and strained to listen again for their howling.

The day before, he had heard the men talking at dinner after morning Meeting. The Hutchinsons always went to Phillip English's for a meal between worship services in Salem Town, and Josiah loved to listen to his father and Phillip English and old Israel Porter discuss the problems of the Massachusetts colony and Salem, Village and Town.

"There is no need for wolf traps and wolf pits anymore, Israel," Josiah's father, Joseph Hutchinson had said—though gently, for he had great respect for his old friend. "In the wolf-rout last year, we barely saw two or three. I can run them off just as easily."

"Aye, until one slaughters one of your cows," old Israel had said.

"Still," Mary English, Phillip's wife, had chimed in, "it does seem cruel, the traps the Putnams set for them."

At the sound of the name "Putnam," Josiah's father's deep-set blue eyes grew dark under his heavy eyebrows. "The Putnams do have a cruel streak," he said. "I always knew they were an ignorant bunch, and not above ignoring a problem if to do so would benefit them. But only of late have I discovered their meanness—"

The conversation then turned from the dangers of wolves in the woods to the dangers of their own neighbors. But now Josiah looked down over sleeping Salem Village and listened once again for the howling. The wolves might be a threat to the farm animals, but Josiah liked to imagine them out there in the Massachusetts woods, skulking among the trees with their sleek, shiny coats and their thick tails, watching, waiting, thinking. It seemed to Josiah that if you could just get to know one, he wouldn't seem so vicious and threatening. If you could just put out your hand for a wolf to lick, or look into his eyes and find out what he was thinking—

In the distance, Josiah heard it again now—a lonely, beseeching howl ringing cleanly through the night. He wanted to throw open the window and howl back. Instead, he crawled quietly into bed.

"Josiah, will you be joining us today, lad?"

Josiah looked up from his reader where the wolves were streaking across the page and stared blankly at his teacher. "Aye, sir—" he said slowly. "I *am* here."

Joseph Putnam chuckled softly. "In body, perhaps, but your mind is—let me see, either out to sea or far up in the woods. Which is it, Captain?"

Josiah felt his cheeks burning, the way they always did when he was caught daydreaming. But Joseph Putnam's eyes twinkled kindly as he turned to the other boys. "Ezekiel, William—what say you? Was Captain Hutchinson with us—or has he escaped the schoolroom without our noticing?"

William Proctor and Ezekiel Porter didn't pounce to answer. Instead, they looked enviously at Josiah. They had only been studying with Joseph Putnam a few weeks. Josiah had had him to himself for the whole summer. Not only was he ahead of them now in reading and numbers, but he and the young teacher were already good friends. To be given a nickname by this sparkly-eyed man with the boyish grin was like having an unexpected present dropped in your lap. Ever since their time together in Salem Town, when Josiah had learned about ships and the sea, Joseph had called him Captain. It was one thing no one ever teased quiet Josiah Hutchinson about.

"Now, then," Joseph said, "since Josiah wants to be out and away anyway, I have a mind to move our studies outside today. What say you to that?"

Three pairs of eyes lit up like candlewicks springing to life, and once again Joseph gave his husky chuckle. "Find a place among the trees, then, and I shall join you presently. And each of you must be ready with a question, eh?"

The early October air was deliciously crisp and filled with the smells of fireplace fires and ripened apples as the three boys burst from Israel Porter's house and tore across the lawn. Until Joseph Putnam married in a few weeks and moved into his own huge, new mansion up on the hill, school for Josiah, Ezekiel, and William was held in old Israel's best room—a wise and somber place that lulled a young boy's brain to either sleep or daydreams by this time in the afternoon. To be outside, racing through the clutter of fallen leaves and chasing squirrels, was like being released from a jail cell— even though Joseph Putnam was like no other teacher they had ever heard of.

Unlike his bitter halfbrothers, Thomas, Nathaniel, Edward, and John, Joseph Putnam was a spirited young man who understood the sometimes-tangled minds of 11-year-old boys. It was too bad, Josiah's father often said, that the "other"

Putnams and their friends in the village refused to allow their children to attend Joseph's school. Since no other education was available in the village, it seemed foolish, he said, to deprive their boys of this chance to learn. But the Putnams, and some other families like them, hated the Hutchinsons, the Porters, the Proctors, and Joseph Putnam himself. They had even prevented them from becoming members of Reverend Parris's church in Salem Village, so that now they had to travel all the way to Salem Town every Sunday to church. To allow their sons to study with them would be something like exposing them to smallpox, Josiah's father would scoff.

But those thoughts were far from the minds of Joseph Putnam's three students as they dove under the leafy umbrella of a red maple and landed in a pile, like squealing puppies. It was Josiah's favorite time of the school day—the time for kicking off his clunky boots, sprawling in the grass on his belly, and asking questions of shiny-eyed Joseph Putnam. There was no question he wouldn't try to answer. In Massachusetts in 1690, that was a rare treat for a Puritan boy.

Joseph stretched out on the ground with them and reached inside his coffee-colored jacket, pulling out three apples and tossing them into the circle. "Now, then," he said, as they scrambled for the apples, "what have you for me today?"

Josiah was the first to raise his hand while the other two began to chomp.

"Captain?"

"Aye—tell us about wolves."

Joseph's eyebrows shot up. "Wolves, Captain?"

"Aye—in the woods. Are they—do they—do we really need to kill them to save our animals?"

"I know only this—" But Joseph's eyes drifted above their heads and his voice trailed off. "What's this now?" he muttered.

The boys turned their heads, and Josiah groaned silently. Nathaniel Putnam was striding importantly down the path that bordered Israel's property, trailed by his tall, lanky son Jonathon. It was easy to tell they were father and son, Josiah always thought. They both had the Putnam large heads and rough-red faces that turned the color of giant radishes when they were angry—which seemed to be most of the time. Now both of them looked at the circle of students and teacher and curled their upper lips.

"Do you see this untidy knot of people?" Nathaniel said to his son, loudly enough for them to hear but pretending he didn't know they could.

"Aye!" Jonathon said just as loudly.

"They call this a school." Nathaniel barked out a laugh. "'Tis not a proper one, though. I see no learning taking place, no discipline—"

"Nay!"

Nathaniel stared hard at all of them. "But 'tis no matter, Jonathon. All the learning a boy needs he can get from his Bible—and *that* he gets in Meetings on Sundays and Lecture Days on Thursdays."

"Good day, Brother Nathaniel!" Joseph Putnam sang out across the yard. His gray-blue eyes were snapping, and the three boys looked at each other, the corners of their mouths twitching. Something delightful was about to happen.

Nathaniel Putnam grunted.

"Come, join us!" cried Joseph. "Bring Jonathon! We are about to discuss one of your favorite subjects!"

"And what might that be?" Nathaniel growled at his half-brother.

"Why wolves, of course!"

Nathaniel's wide face began to redden. Ezekiel nudged Josiah.

"What do I care about wolves, except that they stay away from my pigs?"

"Do you set traps for them, then?" Joseph's eyes were wide and innocent.

"Aye." Nathaniel slanted him a suspicious look. "Why?"

"And what have you caught in your traps—of late, I mean?"

The crimson face was now a shade of purple, and the words burst from his mouth like tiny explosions. "Why—wolves—what else should I catch?"

"Now, that's not what I heard."

Josiah looked curiously at William and Ezekiel, but both of them shrugged. Where was Joseph going with this?

Jonathon closely studied the toe of his boot, while his father blustered on. "What do you mean, Putnam?" Nathaniel cried. "What is it you think you've heard about my wolf traps?"

"I heard only that a tall, two-legged wolf was caught in one of your traps. It must have been a wolf, though—for it was heard howling halfway across Essex County."

"I was caught in it only for a fraction of a second!" Nathaniel screamed, his scarlet face sizzling and his eyes bulging from their sockets.

Beside him, Jonathon Putnam let out a snort. Like a jackrabbit, his father was on him, whacking the side of his head with the back of his hand while still screeching at Joseph. "How dare you, Joseph! How dare you try to—to—make a fool out of me—in the very presence of my son!"

It seemed to Josiah that Jonathon was enjoying the scene as much as they were, although not for long, he was sure. With a wrench of his wrist, Nathaniel took his son by the ear and stomped off down the path. He was still ranting about the evil natures of children when he reached the Ipswich Road and disappeared.

"Well, gentlemen," said Joseph Putnam, his eyes sparkling, "I have told you all I know about wolves. Suppose we go on to other subjects?"

Josiah gave one last look toward the Ipswich Road. As many problems as the Putnams—other than Joseph—had caused for his family, he couldn't help feeling a little bit sorry for Jonathon Putnam. To have a father like that and to be caught snickering at him—Josiah would rather be caught in a wolf trap himself.

✢ ⊹ ✢

chool ended in late afternoon. The air was hazy with smoke from everyone's supper fires and golden with the setting sun.

Josiah felt the glow all around him, like a big halo, as he took a juicy bite out of the apple Joseph Putnam had given him and cut across the Crane Bridge, just below the sawmill his father owned with Israel Porter. He was nearly on the southern border of Salem Village where the houses and farms gave way to the wilderness that led to Salem Town. He was a little nervous being so far from village eyes and voices, but he had come this way to avoid passing Nathaniel Putnam's house. Nathaniel would be fuming for three days—and Josiah wasn't sure he could look at him without snorting himself, thinking of him with his leg caught in his own wolf trap. If Nathaniel Putnam got that angry when his own son laughed at him, there was no telling what he would do to Josiah.

Josiah stopped for a minute to look down into the gray-blue Crane River, one of the many that flowed into Salem Harbor and made for perfect trade of lumber between his father and shipowner Phillip English in Salem Town.

As he looked into the water, Josiah caught his breath. Above him, the New England trees were a sizzling riot of color—the oranges and golds of the oaks, the scarlets and purples of the maples—and they surrounded his face in the water like a dizzily painted picture frame.

"Boy!" said a voice.

Josiah jumped and backed against the bridge railing. At his elbow stood an Indian.

"Boy," the Indian said again.

Josiah nodded, his heart hammering. It took only a moment to see that this was a squaw, and an old one at that. But she *was* an Indian, and Josiah's last meeting with one of the adults of the Algonkian tribe had not been a happy one.

She was short and squatty, and her black head was covered with a bright blue shawl. She was no taller than Josiah, and she looked straight into his eyes, as if waiting for him to answer.

"What?" Josiah said finally.

To his surprise, her brown flat face broke into a smile that crackled with happy lines. "Basket!" she said and pushed an arm-long row of them toward him. They swung merrily by their handles from her wrist to her shoulder.

"Basket?" she said again.

"Oh—no—thank you," Josiah said. "No money."

The squaw's shiny, black eyes went to Josiah's waist, where

a white cloth pouch Hope had made for him swung by a drawstring.

"Oh—no money there," Josiah said. The pouch held only a wooden whistle he'd recently carved and a big bronze-colored leaf he especially liked.

The Indian squaw looked disappointed and a little suspicious, Josiah thought, as she lowered her armful of baskets and turned away. She muttered all the way down the bridge and looked back once as if to make sure he wasn't counting his hidden shillings even now.

"I'm sorry!" Josiah called as she padded off down the road. She turned to look over her shoulder—and she smiled.

When she was out of sight, Josiah strolled over the bridge, finishing off his apple and tossing the core near an oak tree where he knew a squirrel would find it during his next search for nuts. Almost at once, he was lost in thought.

Seeing the old Indian woman had reminded him of two people—Oneko and the Widow Hooker. It was a funny thing about losing people you loved, he decided. He could go for a long time and do the usual things and laugh and feel easy and never really think of them at all. And then suddenly something would jump into his memory and spread the waves like a rock in a calm pool. The achy sadness would come over him again, and he'd miss them.

"Boy!" said a voice behind him.

Josiah froze. It wasn't an Indian this time. It was someone trying to sound like an Indian, and something told Josiah this was even worse.

"Boy!" said a different voice.

Before he could even turn to see who they were, they had him by the arms, one on each side.

"Where are you going, boy?" said Jonathon Putnam on his right.

"Have you a secret meeting with another old Indian woman?" said Eleazer Putnam on his left. Eleazer was John Putnam's son, and although his round, bulbous head was well above Josiah's, he was the same age and a good deal skinnier. It was his grasp that Josiah shook off now. Jonathon was 14 and wiry and harder to get away from.

"Ooh!" Jonathon said as Eleazer stumbled backward. "The little brainless b—b—boy is tough now, eh? He spent a summer in Salem T—T—Town and now he's a b—b—bully."

The dread began to rise in Josiah's stomach. He'd known this was coming for weeks, and now it was time to kick in *the proof*. If he didn't do it now, he might as well go back to being—

Quickly, he jerked his arm to pull away from Jonathon, but the tall boy's grip was firm. He looked down at Josiah with slanted lips and laughed. He had a laugh like a hissing tea kettle.

"Let go of my arm, please," Josiah said.

"Perhaps," Jonathon said. "In time."

Josiah scowled and yanked his arm again. Eleazer stood in front of him and waggled his tongue.

"Wh—wh—what will you do now, b—b—boy?" Jonathon said.

That is the question, isn't it? Josiah thought. He could catch Jonathon by surprise by stomping on his foot and then running. He could promise them something if they'd let him go. He could cry and let them have their fun until they got tired of the game and went home. He knew any of these would work. He'd used them all before—in the days when he himself thought he was a brainless boy.

But now—it was time for *the proof.*

Sighing, he turned to Eleazer, who had added two fingers up his nose to the picture of the waggling tongue.

"What are you doing?" Josiah said without interest. "If you're trying to look like a sick hog, it's working quite well."

Jonathon hissed. "You do, Eleazer," he said. "You put me in mind of a mad sow."

"I don't!" Eleazer shouted, and he kicked at the path and sent a spray of dust into Jonathon's face.

"Bloody mongrel!" Jonathon cried. He dove for Eleazer, letting go of Josiah's arm in the process. Forcing himself not to run, Josiah walked away from them and on down the path.

"Hey!" Jonathon called from behind. "Hey, b—b—boy. Wh—wh—where do you think you're g—g—going?"

Josiah turned and looked closely at Jonathon, squinting his eyes and screwing up his mouth. "Why are you talking that way, Jonathon Putnam?" he said. "I never knew you to stutter."

Jonathon looked at his cousin for a moment and then recovered quickly. He moved closer to Josiah in menacing steps. "I don't stutter, Hutchinson," he said. "I'm imitating you." He stuck out a bony finger to poke it into Josiah's chest, but Josiah pushed it carelessly away.

"I used to stutter when I was around bullies like you," Josiah said. "But if you'll notice, I don't anymore." He shrugged. "I suppose it's because you don't scare me anymore." He looked at Eleazer. "Do you suppose that's it, then?"

Completely stunned, Eleazer shrugged, and Jonathon reached over and whacked him on the side of his very round head, just as Josiah had seen Jonathon's father do to him. Again, Josiah turned and walked away.

"You haven't heard the last of us, Josiah Hutchinson!" Jonathon called after him. "We'll get you for this!"

Josiah wasn't quite sure what it was he was supposed to have done, so he kept walking.

As if in answer, Jonathon shouted, "That pig your father sold us died—two days later!"

"Aye!" Eleazer joined in. "After it destroyed the vegetable garden." He was bolder now that Josiah was well down the path.

"You laughed at my father today! You laughed in his face— and we'll see to that!" That was the last thing Josiah heard Jonathon say as he rounded the curve—and broke into a run.

He didn't stop until he passed his own farm—just in case they thought to follow him there. He stopped at the Training Ground and leaned against the fence to let his breath catch up to him.

Every day, Sergeant Thomas Putnam was here drilling his 24 scouts, to ready them in case the Indians should attack. Even though the Indians had always kept their distance from the villagers, he had spread the word that men working alone in their fields were easy prey for the neighboring tribes and advised them to keep their weapons always near. He even carried his musket to Sabbath Meeting.

As Josiah watched the men marching up and down in ragged rows with Thomas Putnam barking over their heads, he wondered vaguely how any of that would protect them from Indian squaws coming at them with their arms full of baskets.

But then his thoughts wandered back to the "battle" he'd just fought. He was definitely easy prey and probably would be for a long time.

It *was* a good performance, considering it was the first one he'd staged since he'd returned from Salem Town. He hadn't stuttered, not a single time, although he wasn't sure he could get through the whole conversation without at least one stumble. Ever since he'd gotten home and Hope had pointed out that his old habit of getting stuck at least four times in a single sentence had disappeared, he'd heard himself talking smoothly. He didn't talk much, but when he did, the words didn't get hopelessly tangled on his tongue anymore.

But he had dreaded the day when he would meet up with Abigail Williams, the Reverend Parris's niece, or some of the Putnams. They could be cruel people, the kind who shot sparrows and chased chickens—just because they could. Maybe he wasn't a sparrow anymore, but he always had to prove it. There always had to be *the proof.*

Even now, as Josiah began to breathe more easily and trudged toward the farmhouse, he didn't feel like he'd just won a battle. Why had he had to fight in the first place? Did he have to go through the rest of his life constantly proving to people that he wasn't an empty-headed chicken who could be frightened and run off by every fox that came along?

He knew the Putnams. They wouldn't forget that they hadn't won today. He would have to prove himself—over and over and over.

When he opened the front door, his thoughts were erased by the sounds of angry voices in the kitchen. One of them was his father's, which wasn't unusual. His father had a lot to be angry about these days.

But the other one was Hope's—and that turned Josiah's blood to ice water. A Puritan child didn't argue with her parents or find fault with them or even speak around them unless spoken to first. Personally, Josiah had always thought he could get more information by keeping his mouth shut and his ears open. It was harder for Hope to keep from asking her question or offering her opinion, but she was always polite when she did it. Always respectful.

But right now she was shouting just as boldly as her father, and Josiah shrank against the front door and listened nervously.

"There is plenty of work for you to do here!" Papa said. "You've naught to go running off to work in an inn!"

"It's John Proctor's inn, Father!" Hope's voice sounded surprisingly even, like Papa's. "He's your good friend—and his own daughter is working there. I would be working beside Sarah—"

"You can work beside your mother—learning to be a good wife and mother!"

"I *know* how to be that. I could do it with my eyes squeezed shut and both hands tied behind my back."

"Sarah Proctor is working in the inn to help her mother. We all have to have other enterprises besides our farms—you know that—just as I have the sawmill. You help your mother here to keep the farm going—especially with your aunt and your cousin coming here to stay with us. And that is the end of it!"

His "that's final" voice brought the room to silence. Josiah was amazed Papa had let Hope say as much as she had, and he breathed a sigh of relief into the quiet.

But Hope wasn't finished.

"Sarah is having a chance to meet interesting people and see what the world is about, Papa," she said in a quiet, but fearless, voice. "I should like to have that chance, too—"

Josiah squinched his eyes shut and hugged the door.

"You shall have the chance to see the inside of your bed chamber!" Joseph Hutchinson thundered. "Now—enough!"

Josiah heard the stomping of shoes across the worn plank kitchen floor, and then the door was flung open and banged against the hall wall. He plastered himself against the front door to avoid being mowed down as Hope marched past him and up the winding staircase to their room. He had only taken one step forward to watch her go when another set of boots clomped across the kitchen, and the broad-shouldered figure of his father loomed in the doorway.

His piercing blue eyes under the hooded sandy brows sliced through Josiah, but Josiah wasn't sure his father really saw him. He dove away from the door just as Papa wrenched it open and charged into the autumn twilight.

Quietly, Josiah slipped into the kitchen. His mother stood

staring at the door, her face pinched. It softened when she saw her son.

"You heard," she said.

"Aye."

She sighed and brushed her fingers lightly across Josiah's arm. "We must pray for them."

For them? Josiah thought. It seemed to him Hope needed most of the prayers right now. But he nodded, and for a minute his mother tugged at one of his sandy curls, so different from her own hair, which was black like Hope's. She was just like Hope, as he was like his father—except in their ways. Hope and her father, Josiah thought, were like fire. Josiah and his mother were like—

Josiah shook his head. "I'll fetch wood for supper," he said.

What they were like, he hadn't figured out yet. He knew now what he wasn't. It would take some doing to decide who he was.

✝ ◆ ✝

Chapter Three

It didn't occur to Josiah until much later that night to ask about something he'd heard his father say while he was shouting at Hope. The conversation at supper had made him forget to ask at the time.

"You'll go to Joseph Putnam's school only in the morning tomorrow, Josiah," his father said. "You'll come with me in the afternoon to the wolf rout."

Josiah let his spoon clatter to his boat-shaped wooden trencher, and stewed pumpkin splashed silently onto the tabletop.

"If you're as clumsy with a musket as you are with a spoon, perhaps you should stay here, eh?" Papa looked at Josiah with amusement. "You've not been on a wolf drive before, have you, son?"

Josiah shook his head. He hadn't been on one, but he knew what they were, and his heart was sinking.

"It shall be Benjamin Porter and his son Ezekiel and his nephew Giles with us. We'll form a circle in the woods and the wolves will scent us from afar and each one will retreat to the center of the circle. They'll be easy to get to that way."

Josiah nervously ran his finger across the motto carved on the side of his wooden trencher. "In the beginning, God created the heaven and the earth," it read. God created the wolves, too—and now the men were planning to shoot them. If he was Hope, he would have said, "Must I go?" But he remembered this afternoon's shouting match and sighed instead.

"I believe this to be much more humane than the kind of trapping the Putnams are doing," Papa said. "Do you know of it?"

Josiah and his mother shook their heads.

"They've taken to tying together several heavy mackerel hooks and dipping them into melted tallow—the way you do your candles, Deborah."

Mama nodded, but she clutched her throat.

"When they've hardened into a bunch," Papa went on, "the hooks can't be seen. They scent them with some kind of food and tie them up with a chain. The wolf, they claim, jumps up at the scent and likes the taste of the tallow, so he—swallows the hooks." Papa's voice grew soft but his eyes hardened. "The chain pulls loose but the wolf is left with the bunch of hooks in his throat. He runs off, only to die in the woods."

"How cruel!" Mama said.

"Aye," said Papa. "The only Putnam family not using that kind of trap is Edward's."

"Well, that's to his credit."

But Papa shook his head. "Nay. The only reason is that if the wolf goes out and dies in the woods, his boys can't claim the bounty, and their names won't go on the town list as having wolf money set to their credit."

Josiah set down his spoon.

"But I'm convinced there aren't many wolves out there anymore," Papa said. It seemed to Josiah he forced his voice to be lighter. "They're shy, the wolves. They don't like us human animals. The more of us there are, the farther away they roam. But—" He looked at Josiah. "We must protect what crops and animals we have left after the locusts and the dry summer. The sawmill is doing well, and my trade with Phillip English will bring us great returns soon, I pray. But we must feed this family in the meantime, eh?"

Mama nodded, but Josiah pushed his trencher away. He didn't feel like feeding himself right now.

When he heard the wolves that night, Josiah ran to the window. He wanted to fling it open and shout to them, "Run! Run away—as far away as you can!"

As it was, he did shove the window panels back and lean out to listen. The frost-tinged autumn air rushed in.

"Close that window!" Hope hissed from her bed.

Josiah ignored her. On the edge of the night, he heard the howling again.

The bed curtains were flung back, and Hope slapped her feet across the room and yanked the windows shut.

"What are you doing?" she said.

"Listening to the wolves."

Hope rolled her eyes and slapped her feet back toward her bed.

Outside, the thin howling started again. It made Josiah lonely, and he wanted Hope to stay up with him—talk to him—about anything. That's when he remembered the question he'd wondered about.

"Are our aunt and cousin really coming here to stay?" he asked. "I heard Papa say—"

Hope whirled around, and for a minute Josiah thought maybe it would have been better to stay lonely. Her eyes, red-rimmed from crying, blazed at him.

"Don't mention Papa to me!" she snapped.

"But what about—"

"In fact, don't mention our aunt and our cousin to me, either—because they're part of the reason I can't go and work at the Proctors' inn with Sarah. Their coming here means more work for me—cooking and washing and all of it."

"But who are they? Why are they coming here?"

He'd learned long ago that whatever Hope said she didn't want to talk about was good for at least a 30-minute conversation.

Hope slapped her way back to the window and plopped down on the trunk next to Josiah. "It's Aunt Esther," she said. "Papa's sister. She was married to Daniel Hawkes when you and I were just babies, and they've always lived in Hingham until they went up to Maine when Uncle Daniel joined the militia. That's why we never saw them. Now Uncle Daniel's been killed in Maine fighting in the Indian wars, and Aunt Esther is in trouble because—oh, I don't know, it's just confusing. The fact is, she's coming here so Papa can help her."

"And the cousin?"

"It's a girl. Her name's Rebecca."

"How old—"

"She's younger than you by a year—and we're to help take care of her since she's upset by her father's death."

Josiah nodded thoughtfully. It would be better, of course, if she were a boy. Girls were so hard to understand most of the time. But it would be good to have another child in the house. In a Puritan home where so much was stiff and somber and ordered by rules made by adults, every child was a partner who helped ease the way.

"She'll be another friend," Josiah said.

Hope snorted and flounced back to bed. "She'll be more work, and I'll be the one doing it!" And with a jerk, she pulled her bed curtains closed.

Josiah looked glumly out the window. He remembered a time when Hope had seemed to hate him. She had called him brainless boy more than anyone else. But then they came to understand each other, and they were friends. Most of the time he was her extra set of ears. She only heard about half of what was said around her since she'd suffered from the fever last spring. Now she was mad again and closing him out.

Josiah sighed and padded to his cot. This time he knew she wasn't mad at him, but that didn't make it any easier. Having another young person in the house could only help— even if she *was* a girl.

During a rare quiet moment in the schoolroom the next day, as Ezekiel hunched over his numbers and William poked his white-blond hair into spikes while he struggled to decipher his reader, Joseph Putnam tapped Josiah softly on the shoulder and beckoned him into the hall.

"Something troubling you today, Captain?" Joseph asked.

Josiah looked at the floor, the ceiling, and each of the walls before he answered. "It's the wolves," he said finally.

"Ah—those creatures again. They're figuring into your thoughts a good deal of late, eh?"

"Aye. I hear them at night, howling, and I feel—I feel like they're lonely."

Now that was stupid, Josiah thought. *He'll think me the village idiot for certain.*

But Joseph nodded slowly, as if carefully considering Josiah's words.

"I've often thought about the way the wolves sound, too," he said at last. "But I don't think they sound lonely. I think they sound—misunderstood."

"Misunderstood?"

"Aye. They're bewildered because we human animals don't seem to realize that they're shy—and that they only come down to the village because they're hungry. With so many of us here now, we're getting to their dinner before they are. We take the squirrels with our muskets—and what have they to do but come down and capture a chicken or two of ours, eh?" His eyes shone softly down at Josiah. "You don't want to come to the wolf rout and take them down, do you, Captain?"

Josiah shook his head. "Papa once said he'd rather just

scare them off, too—but now he's talking of muskets. I don't understand."

Joseph put an arm around his shoulders. "I'm a believer in surprises," he said. "And I think we may see a surprise out there in the woods today."

Josiah felt his eyes widening. "We?"

"Aye. I have a place of my own to keep up. I must be a part of this wolf business, too, then. Now—back to *WINGATE'S ARITHMETIC* before your father finds another teacher, eh?"

It was funny, Josiah decided later as he gazed down at a page of sums. You could feel so low your tongue scraped the ground, and then the right person said the right thing and—snap!—your tongue was in your mouth again, and you were even smiling.

But the closer they came to Fair Maid's Hill that afternoon, the less Josiah was smiling. It was because of the musket his father was carrying.

All the men—Ezekiel's father, Benjamin Porter; Papa; and Joseph Putnam—had hoisted their heavy iron and wood muskets over their shoulders when they left the Hutchinson farm. Benjamin and Ezekiel had headed in one direction, Giles and Joseph in another, and Josiah and his father in still another, so that they could form a sort of triangle in the large meadow near Fair Maid's Hill. The horn holding the gunpowder bounced at Joseph Hutchinson's waist as he walked, and Josiah stared at it gloomily. Perhaps this was better than the hook traps the Putnams used, but he still didn't see why they had to kill the wolves at all. The only thing that kept him from running back to the farm was what Joseph Putnam had said—that they would see a surprise.

They stopped at the foot of the gently sloping hill, and Papa took the musket from his shoulder to load it. Josiah shivered when he looked at it. He had never liked the looks of guns. The barrel was long, and the front flared out like a trumpet. Along the side and toward the back was what Papa had told him was the hammer. When Papa pulled the trigger, it would strike a piece of flint to set off the black powder inside and explode it, firing the gun. Ezekiel thought muskets were exciting. All Josiah could think of were the wolves.

Papa emptied a small amount of black powder from the horn into the front of the gun and then used the long wooden piece attached to the barrel to push a piece of wadded-up cloth inside. Then he pushed an iron ball in with another piece of wadding that would keep it in. As he worked, he talked in a quiet voice to Josiah.

"Even now," he said, "the wolves—if indeed there are any—will smell us and begin to move to the center of our triangle. Then we can see them and decide what to do to keep the critters from disturbing our cattle, eh?"

Josiah didn't answer.

Papa leaned in close to him. "You must trust my judgment, Josiah."

Josiah nodded unhappily.

Papa put the musket up to his shoulder and looked down its long, narrow barrel. Josiah looked quickly in the same direction, but then Papa lowered the musket and settled himself behind a rock. "Now we wait," he said.

Josiah slumped to the ground next to his father and looked around. Straight to the east, along the marsh that bordered Crane Brook, he thought he spotted Giles and Joseph. He looked north, but he couldn't find Ezekiel and his father. At this very moment, Ezekiel was probably begging his father to let him hold the musket, just for a minute.

"Ah," Papa said softly.

Josiah followed his father's eyes to the meadow that stretched before them. From out of the trees came a sleek animal in a coat of every shade of gray. It was the first wolf Josiah had ever seen, and he held his breath as he watched him tear across the field and stop at its center to sniff the air. The most beautiful thing about him was his tail, Josiah decided at once. It was thick, and it shone behind him as the sun hit it.

"He smells us," Papa whispered.

It took every bit of control Josiah had not to cry out, "Run! Run for your life!"

But the wolf looked mixed up enough already. He ran first to the north, where Ezekiel and his father were crouched. Then he skittered fearfully to the east, where Joseph's gun would be pointed at him.

And then, confused by the bewildering circle of scents, the wolf came straight toward where Josiah and his father squatted behind the rock. Josiah felt tears gathering.

For there, just six feet from them, Josiah could see the look in the wolf's eyes—a wild look of almost paralyzed fear.

The wolf was well within range now, and Josiah watched his father raise the musket and put its stock against his chest. In the stillness of the autumn afternoon, he heard the hammer cock back. It was about to happen. His father was going to shoot the wolf.

Josiah couldn't watch, and he turned his head toward his father.

That's when he saw the promised surprise. Papa pulled the gun barrel up—and up—and up until it pointed straight toward the sky. He squeezed the trigger with his finger, and the air came alive with its explosive bang. Another shot came from across the meadow, and another to the north, all into the air, and not at the wolf.

Josiah whipped his head toward the wolf, but the frightened animal had finally chosen a direction and sprinted toward the woods now with his ears pulled back in sheer terror.

The unfriendly burning smell of the gunpowder fell like a cloud over Josiah, and his ears were ringing from the blast—but he was smiling.

"I think that ought to scare him off for a while," Papa said. "What say you to a cup of cider in our kitchen, eh?"

"Aye, sir," Josiah said, and he even offered to carry the empty musket home.

✢ ✢ ✢

Chapter Four

osiah! Josiah—wake up! Are you deaf, too? Wake up! They're here!"

Josiah blinked his heavy eyelids open and stared at Hope. She was crouched on the edge of his bed, shaking his shoulders with both hands.

"The wolves?" He sat straight up on his cot. "The wolves are here?"

"Have you gone mad with this wolf business?" Hope said. "No—Aunt Esther and Cousin Rebecca are here! Get up now!"

She pulled a cloak around her nightdress and slipped out the door. Still thick with sleep, Josiah looked around the dark room. *It's the middle of the night,* he thought. *Why must people arrive in the middle of the night?*

Hope poked her head back in the room. "Come on, then!"

Josiah pushed back his quilt and stumbled, bleary-eyed,

down the stairs and into the kitchen. A fire blazed in the fireplace, and Josiah went straight to it. The air was chilly and the floorboards were cold under his bare feet.

"Josiah," Mama said softly, "this is your Aunt Esther."

Josiah searched the kitchen for a stranger and found her huddled in Papa's chair near the fire. Josiah's brain leapt awake as he looked at her. If there could be a female version of his father, she was it. Aunt Esther had the same sandy curls and the same square jaw as Papa. Even her shoulders were broad and proud. Only her eyes were different—they were blue but not sharp and bright like Papa's. They were puffy and faded, as if months of tears had washed the color away.

Suddenly, Josiah felt shy. He didn't often meet new people here in the village, and this lady's husband had just died. What did you say to someone whose sadness seemed to wrap around her like a blanket?

"How do you do, Josiah?" Her voice was as colorless as her eyes, as if she had nothing left to feel.

Josiah nodded and muttered something like "Aye."

"Josiah," Papa said, nudging him, "you might have come downstairs in something other than your nightshirt."

Josiah looked blankly down at himself. The loose muslin shirt's bottom barely covered his. He felt his cheeks begin to burn.

But Aunt Esther didn't seem to notice his almost-nakedness. She turned to Mama and held out her hands. "You're so kind to take us in, Deborah. I promise you we won't trouble you for long, Rebecca and I. As soon as Joseph can help us settle Daniel's estate, we shall be on our way."

Softly, Josiah's mother went to her side, and Josiah looked around the kitchen again. He'd almost forgotten about his cousin Rebecca, who was sitting beside his sister at the table. Her arms were sprawled straight out in front of her across the tabletop, one of them draped over a lumpy cloth and straw doll. Her face lay sideways between her arms, and her cheek was pressed against the wood as she slept heavily. Hope looked up at Josiah and wiggled her eyebrows. Ten-year-old Rebecca Hawkes was snoring like a bear.

"It shouldn't take us long, once I've figured out how to go about it," Papa was saying. "But that isn't the point, Esther. The point is that you are family, and you are welcome in this house for as long as you need to be here."

"Aye," Mama said quietly.

"It seems so unfair, the way things must be done," Aunt Esther said. "We must go all the way to Boston to settle it—that's the rule of the governor. And when I get there, what shall I do? I don't understand how—I cannot read their instructions—"

"You need not travel to Boston, sister," Papa said. "I have friends in Salem Town—men of learning and importance who can show us the way. 'Tis a pity things are such as they are, though," he said as Mama put a mug of warmed cider into his hand and cradled one in Aunt Esther's, too. Papa drank it gratefully, but Esther cupped her hands around hers and stared into it dully as if she didn't know what to do with it. Josiah thought she must have forgotten how to do anything but worry.

"Papa always talked of Massachusetts as God's own colony," Joseph Hutchinson went on. "He and the others came here to create their ideal state, without interference. But ever since our champion in England died, ever since Oliver Cromwell died and Charles II came to the throne, that has been almost impossible." He put down his mug and leaned toward Aunt Esther to look at her closely, as if he could make her understand with his eyes, Josiah thought. "Twenty-six years ago that king sent a commission here to the colony with orders to assert royal power over us. Since then, it seems, there has been one disaster after another. Wars with the Indians, fighting amongst ourselves—and then the taking away of our charter six years ago. Y'see, that's why this settling of Daniel's estate is so difficult, Esther—because we are now under the rule of a royal governor."

"But was he not overthrown last year?" Esther asked. "Daniel did tell me that."

"Aye, Governor Andros was a tyrant. He's the one responsible for the rule that you must go to Boston to do business with the government—and he raised the fees for doing so to the highest they have ever been. The colonists in Boston did indeed tear him from office, but now things are even worse, if that is indeed possible. Old Simon Bradstreet is in office now, but he can do nothing, either for or against us. Increase Mather has been in England three years now, trying to get a new charter for us from King James to replace the one King Charles revoked. And in the midst of that, King James himself was replaced by William and Mary, which has made progress there even more unlikely because they are unhappy with the overthrowing of Andros by the colonists. We are in between—we have no real government, no real charter, not even a real governor."

Aunt Esther covered her face with her hands, but Papa reached out and took both of her wrists and pulled them away from her eyes. "You cannot despair, Esther," he said. "Perhaps my good friends in Salem Town and I can use this tangle in Boston to our advantage, eh? In the midst of the confusion, we may be able to slip between the rules. That's what I intend."

Esther Hawkes put her hands up to hold Joseph's wrists. "You have always been such a kind brother to me," she said. "God bless you."

They're brother and sister, Josiah thought, *just as Hope and I are.* He went to the table and, like Rebecca, put his head down on the top. *I wonder if they had the same kinds of secrets and adventures that Hope and I have,* he thought. He glanced at Hope now as she left the kitchen to prepare a bed in the sitting room where Aunt Esther and Rebecca would be staying. *I wonder if Papa understood his sister any better than I do mine. Why do they get so angry and snap at the whole world like a cornered rattlesnake?* Josiah looked sleepily at Rebecca. Strings of acorn-colored hair hung limply from her cap, and a tiny stream of drool trailed from the corner of her mouth as she snored on in grunts and puffs. She looked so young to be ten, but at least she was another child, another possible friend. In this world of confusion, he could use all the friends he could find.

Josiah's eyelids grew heavy again, and they had almost slammed shut when his father's words brought them open.

"I am not saying that Daniel's fighting the Indians was wrong," Papa said. "When our communities are attacked, of course we must fight back."

"Then, what are you saying?" Aunt Esther said tearfully. "Our house and barn in Maine were burned, Joseph! We barely escaped with our lives. If it weren't for Daniel's property in Hingham, Rebecca and I would be beggars."

"I am saying that there would be no attacks if the white man had handled his relationship with the Indians properly in the first place. We started out the right way. Captain John Alden of Plymouth had a truce with the Indians. The colony was living in peace with them. And then people became greedy. Traders and land buyers broke the truce and took their land. Why wouldn't they become angry? And, of course, the French in northern New England—they have pushed the Indians to attack those settlements so they can have them for themselves. And these old-guard Puritans in Boston who are trying to run Governor Bradstreet—they are doing nothing to help the colonists in Maine."

Papa began to pace around the kitchen, looking out windows and running his big, rough hands through his hair. Josiah watched him carefully. These were the times when his silent questions were answered.

"The thing that is most troublesome to me is that it is all done in the name of God," Papa said. "There were those Puritans who came here and looked at this New World as the devil's territory, and they saw the Indians as the devil's people. They thought they were here to tame it—so they saw nothing wrong with stealing land from the Indians." Goodman Hutchinson shook his head sadly. "That is not what our father came to this wilderness to see, Esther. And for our part of it, I would rather befriend our Indian brothers and respect their dignity than shoot them down in cold blood because they're attacking us in anger at things we did to them in the first place." To Josiah's surprise, his father's eyes came to rest on him. "That is why I insist that Josiah be well educated, and why Hope, too, has learned to read and write. They must know this world if they are to do God's will in it." His hard-lined face softened a little as he looked down at the snoozing Rebecca. "Perhaps we can see that my niece receives a little instruction while she's here, eh?"

"Oh—I don't think so!" Aunt Esther said quickly.

Everyone in the kitchen looked at her curiously. She was gnawing at her lip, and her hands became suddenly restless.

"Come now, Esther," Joseph Hutchinson said. "Are you one of these stiff-necked Puritans who believe that a person must only trust God and never do anything to use the gifts God has given her?"

Aunt Esther's eyes darted helplessly around the room. "No," she said. "I just don't think Rebecca would be able—" She stopped and sighed. "I am so tired now. Can we not talk of this tomorrow?"

"Of course," Mama said. And in one of her rare moments of decision, she swept Esther out of the kitchen and up the stairs. "Will you carry Rebecca up?" she said over her shoulder.

Josiah and his father both looked down at the sleeping girl whose cheek was now pushed out of shape against the tabletop.

"This girl has seen a lot of trouble and sorrow, Josiah," Papa said. "You must help erase that from her mind, eh?"

"Aye."

When Goodman Hutchinson lifted his niece up onto his

shoulder, the lumpy poppet with its yarn hair and lopsided smile toppled to the floor. Josiah picked it up and looked at it. Its face was spotted with yellowish stains.

"I think you've seen a lot of trouble and sorrow, too," Josiah said.

"Talking to dolls now, are you?" Hope said from the doorway. "Mama says to come to bed."

Josiah looked up at his sister, who was laughing into the sleeve of her nightdress. He made a face at the doll and slung it over his shoulder.

✝ ✦ ✝

osiah," Hope called from the ground, "get those high branches. You can climb higher than the rest of us."

"I can climb just as high. Let me get them!" Ezekiel reached a long, lanky arm to the limb above his head and swung himself up.

"You cannot either, Ezekiel Porter!" his sister Rachel barked. "Every time you try, you drop like a stone."

"Do not!"

Josiah made his way to the highest branches and began to pick the last of this year's apples and stuff them into the basket he had strung close by. It would be a while before they would expect him on the ground again. They were too busy bickering and trying to outpick each other in apples and wild pears and nuts. Hope wanted this to last as long as possible anyway, he knew. She wasn't looking forward to slicing and peeling and drying the apples and pressing the pears for cider. She'd even muttered to Josiah yesterday that she was glad Papa's corn crop was ruined by locusts last summer so she wouldn't have to sit and husk corn for hours. The longer he stayed up here, the longer he could be away from her simmering anger.

The top of a tree, any tree, was where Josiah liked to be the most. And Hope was right about one thing. Ever since Oneko, his Indian friend, had taught him some climbing tricks last spring, he could climb higher than any of them.

As he popped the shiny apples from the branches and dropped them in the basket, Josiah looked down at Salem Village below him. It was still early, and the movement of the cows and goats and the few villagers who were out and about was still sleepy and slow. The motion of something bright blue to the north caught his eye, and he leaned into the branch to get a better look.

He let out a soft gasp. It was an Indian—skulking there among the trees. Josiah looked down at the Porters and Hope. They were all alone out here, outside of shouting distance from the farmhouse. People said Salem Village was especially open to Indian attacks because it was so spread out. And even his father had said the Indians were angry—

"Boy!" said a voice.

Josiah sank against the branch in relief and laughed out loud. It was the old squaw, still swinging her row of baskets over her arm, still wearing the bright blue shawl over her head.

"Squaw!" he said back to her.

"Josiah, who are you talking to?" Rachel shouted.

Josiah looked down at the squaw. She'd bent her knees

and spread out her arms, and she was staring in the direction of Rachel's voice with caution in her eyes.

"It's all right," Josiah whispered. "They're friends."

"What's he saying?" he heard Hope say.

"I thought he said, 'Squaw'!" Rachel said.

"It's all right," Josiah said again. But when he looked, the squaw was gone.

Quickly, he twisted his neck to look around, but the only movement came from the direction of the farmhouse. A stocky little girl was stumbling clumsily amid the rocks toward the orchard. Her hair was streaming behind her, and she was lugging something that bumped and bounced along the ground at her ankles.

"Hope!" he cried. "Who's that coming from the house?"

"What?"

"He said who's that coming from your house!" Ezekiel called from another tree.

"I can't hear—"

"From your house! Someone's coming!" Rachel called.

By the time Hope got the word, the staggering little figure had reached the edge of the orchard. She stared up at Josiah, mouth hanging open and eyes wide as a codfish's.

"Oh!" he heard Hope say. "You must be Rebecca."

Their aunt and cousin were still in bed when they had tiptoed downstairs this morning to do their chores. There was no school today, the day before the Sabbath, and there was too much to do for them to be allowed to wait for their new family members to wake up. Mama said they had traveled for days and might even sleep that long.

Josiah hung farther out on the branch to get a closer look at his cousin. She was a square little person who looked even shorter now that she was awake. Sturdy stock, Papa would have said.

Hope crouched beside her now to talk to her, and Rebecca stared at her, mouth still gaping just as it had when she was snoring on the table last night. There was something at the side of her mouth, and Josiah leaned just a little farther out to see it. The next thing he knew, he was on his back on the ground, looking up at her and hauling in breath.

"This is your cousin Josiah," Hope said slyly. "He's the best tree climber in Essex County."

"You fell down," Rebecca said loudly. She truly did look impressed, however, and she swung her lumpy doll behind her shyly as she continued to stare down at him.

Josiah stared back. Just as he'd thought, a thin stream of drool had puddled at the corner of her mouth. *Doesn't she ever close it?* he wondered.

"Would you like to help us pick apples and pears, Rebecca?" Hope said kindly.

Rebecca nodded as if just that took all her concentration. Behind her, Rachel looked up at Ezekiel and opened her eyes wide. Ezekiel shrugged and went back to picking.

"You've done it before, haven't you?" Hope said.

With just as much effort, Rebecca shook her head. Rachel rolled her eyes and took her basket to another tree.

"I suppose I'll have to show you how, then, eh?" Hope said. "It's easy, really. Go and get yourself a basket."

She pointed to several in a pile nearby, and Rebecca

grinned happily and took off after them like a jackrabbit. In two steps she was sprawled on the ground, still clutching the doll.

"Oh, my, are you hurt?" Hope rushed over to help her cousin up, and Josiah himself scrambled from the ground and back up the tree.

"I fell down," Rebecca said.

Even from the top branch Josiah could hear her. In fact, they could probably hear her in Topsfield. She had a voice that bleated like their calf.

"Now," he heard Hope saying, "can you climb a tree?"

Rebecca slowly shook her head.

"All right, then, you shall take care of the lower branches, eh? Just stand on tiptoes."

Rebecca held the basket straight out to one side and the doll straight out to the other side and tried to get up on her toes the way Hope was showing her. Both arms flailed while the doll went sailing through the air, and the basket came squarely down on the top of Hope's head.

Below him, Ezekiel buried his mouth in his hand and snorted. At the far tree, Josiah saw Rachel's shoulders shaking. Josiah climbed one branch higher.

"Let's try that again," Hope said tightly. Josiah could almost hear her teeth gritting.

Within an hour it became obvious that Rebecca was not cut out for apple and pear picking. But she did seem to have a talent for following, and she stayed on Hope's heels, close enough to tromp up the back of them most of the time, all the while mooing loudly and happily. Hope had only collected half a basket of fruit, and she finally glared up into the sun in Josiah's direction.

"Perhaps Josiah should show you how to climb a tree so you can pick higher," she shouted, more for his benefit than for Rebecca's, he was sure. "You would do that for your cousin, wouldn't you, Josiah?"

"Wouldn't you, Josiah?" Ezekiel repeated in a high, squeaky voice.

"Shut it, Ezekiel!" Hope said.

If she hadn't sounded ready to rip the head off any passing sparrow, and if Papa hadn't said they were supposed to help erase Rebecca's trouble and sorrow, Josiah would have stayed safely in the top of the tree. But he came down a few branches and dropped to the ground next to Rebecca. She looked up at him with wide, wondering blue eyes. They were the same color as Papa's, and he could see his own reflection in their shine.

He looked at her stubby little legs, doubtfully. They weren't made for tree climbing.

"You can carry my basket for me," he said.

She made a move to dive for it, but Josiah stuck out his arm to stop her. She ran into it and toppled heavily to the ground.

"Enjoy," Hope said through a frozen smile and hurried off to join Rachel.

"I fell down," Rebecca said.

"So I see." Josiah stuck his hand down to her, and she grabbed it in a clammy paw and pulled herself up. He was surprised at how solid she was. She felt like ten, but she didn't look like it, and she surely didn't act like it. She seemed to have the mind of someone much younger. Sighing, Josiah picked up his basket and held it out to her. "You take one handle, and I'll take the other. We're going to that tree—"

But before he could point, she had trudged off happily, basket handle in hand—in the wrong direction.

"Okay," he muttered. "We can go to that tree."

"That would be the perfect tree," Ezekiel hissed from above.

Josiah discovered two things in the time between his takeover of Rebecca and dinner. Both of them he learned when the pigeons flew over.

They had managed to get the basket to a tree far from everyone else, and Josiah had convinced Rebecca that standing next to the basket while he filled it was "helping," when the sky had suddenly darkened as if they were about to have a thunderstorm. It always happened when the flocks of passenger pigeons migrated in the fall. Papa had once said there were more than a billion birds in the sky at one time, and they could turn the day into night in minutes.

Josiah was only a few branches up, and when he heard the thunderous cooing, he looked down at Rebecca. Her already-wide eyes were popping as she stared, stricken, at the sky. The shadow of the birds that passed over her face couldn't match the shadow of pure fear that covered it first.

"It's just the pigeons!" Josiah shouted.

He looked up and watched them as they passed over in a giant wave of dark wings and russet tummies. It was something he waited for every fall, and he couldn't help cooing up to them as they traveled overhead.

And then he heard a cooing from below. *Has one of the pigeons fallen from the sky?* he wondered.

He scrambled down from the tree and looked around. Rebecca still stood, stock-still, her eyes glued to the now-lightening sky.

There it was again—the cooing on the ground. Josiah turned and saw Rebecca, lips in an "o," making a perfect pigeon sound.

"Aye!" Josiah said. "You sound just like one of them!"

In answer, she hooted in his face.

"That's—that's amazing," he said.

She just kept cooing.

"Can you make any other sounds?"

She cocked her head. "I don't know," she said loudly.

Josiah looked around. Not far from them, a squirrel was about to do its shopping in a walnut tree. "There," Josiah whispered. "Can you sound like a squirrel?"

"Where?" she bleated.

The squirrel scampered up the tree, chittering nervously. Rebecca chittered, too. The squirrel stopped and turned its head toward her.

"Do it again!" Josiah whispered.

Rebecca chattered, blank-faced. The squirrel ran right toward them.

So those were the two things Josiah learned about his cousin. Like a five-year-old, she was easily terrified, to the point of being frozen to the ground. And she could imitate any animal in the New England countryside. By dinnertime, she had mocked an owl, a dove, a woodpecker, and a meadow mouse.

"You certainly haven't done much picking," Hope said to him as they headed toward the house for dinner.

Josiah looked down at Rebecca whose jerky steps were bouncing the basket she was helping him carry and bruising the fruit they had managed to get out of the trees.

"It isn't easy." Josiah nodded toward their cousin.

Hope rolled her eyes and leaned forward to look at Rebecca. "Perhaps you should rest at home after dinner," Hope said to her. "You must be tired from your trip."

"I'm helping Joshua!" she said loudly and happily. It was difficult for her to answer and manage the basket at the same time, and her steps faltered and she spilled to the ground again. She pulled herself up slowly and went after her doll. Hope snatched Josiah by the arm and yanked him aside. Her words fizzed hotly in his ear.

"I'm going to have to teach her *everything*!" she said. "She can't do *anything*!"

"She can imitate any animal—"

"What good is that?" Hope watched Rebecca waddle toward them with her doll, and she pulled Josiah closer by the collar. "I am *not* going to do it, Josiah! Do you hear me? I am *not* going to do it. It's bad enough being stuck here working on the farm instead of getting out like you do—and like Sarah Proctor. But I will *not* play nursemaid to that—that—"

"Joshua," Rebecca said. "I fell down, but I'm ready now."

"Besides," Hope said as she swept up her skirts and turned to go. "It seems she has chosen you."

Rebecca looked up at Josiah with adoring eyes and slipped her chunky hand into his. With a jerk, he pulled it away.

"Come along," he said.

"All right, Joshua."

"Josiah," he said through gritted teeth. "Josiah."

✝ ⬦ ✝

Chapter Six

osiah discovered one more thing about his cousin
Rebecca before the week was out.

It was the third day in a row now that she had met him
in the barn before dawn, even before he went to school.
She'd stumble in while he was milking the cow or tossing hay
from the hayloft, dragging her doll and watching him with
both her eyes and her mouth wide—and she would ask him
questions.

"Why do you do that, Joshua? What is that for, Joshua?
Will that hurt you, Joshua?"

At first he tried to answer her questions, but one answer
always seemed to lead to another question.

"Why do you climb up there?" she asked when he went up
into the hayloft.

"To get hay for the oxen," he said.

"Why?"

47

"So they can eat it."

"Why?"

That was the day an answer came out of his mouth that stopped her cold.

"So they won't eat *you*!" he said.

Immediately, Rebecca was frozen to the barn floor, and her pale blue eyes shimmered with fear.

"Eat—eat me?" she said finally.

Josiah pitched a forkful of hay out of the loft and thought where to go from there. She looked up at him, waiting for the wisdom from above.

"Nay," he said. "Not if you stay away from them."

She let out a noisy sigh of relief and sank down on top of the pile of hay. Josiah didn't see her, and the next forkful landed on her head. She screamed until he came down and brushed it out of her face.

"Thank you, Joshua!" she said as gratefully as if he'd saved her life. Tears were poised at the edges of her lower lids.

She must believe everything I tell her, Josiah thought.

That proved to be true the very next day, when to his horror she met him at the door of the schoolroom when class was over for the day.

"Good day, Joshua!"

"How did you get here?" Josiah demanded.

She turned and pointed down the dark hall where his father stood in the doorway talking to old Israel Porter.

"Oh," Josiah said.

"And who would this lovely visitor be?" Joseph Putnam said behind him.

Immediately, Rebecca dove behind Josiah and peeked out from behind his vest. Beside Josiah, Ezekiel snickered and slid past him with William Proctor in tow.

"Good day, Joshua!" he said, and they slithered down the hall, giggling.

"This is my cousin Rebecca," Josiah muttered.

Joseph Putnam squatted and peeked around Josiah to have a look at her. Shyly, she peeked back. Joseph reached out and ran a finger lightly over the doll's arm.

"And who might this be?" he asked.

"E-liz-a-beth," she said in her too-loud voice.

"Beautiful name," Joseph said. "She is almost as pretty as you are. Did you know that?"

Rebecca shook her head slowly, but Josiah saw a smile twitching at the corners of her droopy mouth.

Joseph stood up and patted Josiah's shoulder. "Has your cousin here begun to teach you to read, Rebecca?"

Rebecca shook her head again and Josiah started shaking his, too.

"He'd best be about it, then, eh?" Joseph said.

"Oh—I can't do that—I—I don't know how to teach someone—"

Josiah stopped. Joseph's kind, shiny eyes were squinting at him, and then his smile hardened and he shrugged and moved away.

"As you wish," he said.

As he walked down the hall toward his father, Josiah had a cold feeling. When Rebecca slipped her hand into his, he pulled away.

"Ah, Josiah," Papa said when he saw him. "I must stay here with Israel Porter and try to work out a way to help your aunt—and we've some other business to attend to. Will you see that your cousin gets home safely?"

Everyone seemed to be looking at him at once—his father, old Israel, Rebecca herself—and Joseph.

"Aye," he mumbled.

Rebecca grabbed his hand again, and he didn't pull away until they were out of sight of the house. Josiah walked hard and fast over the bridge, and Rebecca trotted along behind him to keep up.

"Where are we going?" she asked.

"Home."

"Why are we going this way?"

"Because it's faster."

"Why are we in a hurry?"

Josiah stopped so quickly, she rammed into the back of him. He turned to face her, bringing his nose very close to hers.

"Because—there are bandits in these woods." He wiggled his eyebrows.

"What—what are 'ban-dits'?" she said nervously.

Josiah hunched his shoulders and looked over both with slanted eyes before he answered. "They're bad boys who like to—like to chase little girls—and—" He groped in his mind for something delicious, and his eyes fell on Elizabeth. "And steal their dolls!"

Rebecca clutched her doll to her chest and breathed hard. Her eyes bulged from her head.

"That's why we have to hurry," he said.

She nodded wildly and grabbed for his hand. He dodged it and turned to run. But three feet away stood Jonathon and Eleazer Putnam. Lurking behind them was their cousin Richard, Thomas Putnam's 12-year-old son.

"Bandits!" Rebecca screamed.

She hurled herself against Josiah's back and locked her arms around his waist. Elizabeth swung between his legs. Inside, Josiah moaned. It was time for more *proof*. Over and over and over again.

"Oh, Josiah!" Jonathon wailed in a too-loud voice. "Save me from the bandits. Save me!"

Like a magpie, Eleazer joined in. Richard just glowered at Josiah and began to circle.

"You're right to be frightened," Jonathon said to Rebecca. "We *are* bandits. *Dangerous* bandits!"

Rebecca's chunky arms tightened around Josiah's waist and cut off his air supply.

"But your mistake is in trusting this brainless boy to protect you."

Jonathon poked a finger into Josiah's chest. Josiah grabbed it and pushed it away.

"Oh, you see, he thinks he's mighty brave," Jonathon said.

"Aye," said Eleazer, not to be left out. "Brave enough to keep company with Indians." He spit out a laugh. "Aye—an old squaw!"

From behind them, Richard grunted, and Josiah felt Rebecca turn to look at him before she reglued her eyes to Jonathon.

"Even if he were brave," Jonathon went on, "he isn't smart —and that's where you're in trouble if you depend on him—"

"He is smart!" Rebecca's voice rang out in the woods and stopped even Richard in his threatening circle. "Joshua knows everything!"

There was only a second's worth of stunned silence before the three Putnam boys erupted in uncontrollable laughter. Richard snickered and clutched his belly, and Eleazer grabbed at his cousin's shirt and gasped for air. Jonathon went down on his knees and hissed like a pit full of vipers.

Josiah saw his chance and, peeling Rebecca's arms from around his waist, he pulled her by the arm all the way to the farm, the laughter still ringing in his ears. When they arrived, her eyes were shiny with tears and she was looking up at him, her mouth gaping.

"You saved me," she said.

"I did not," Josiah growled.

"Aye, you did. Those bandits—"

They aren't bandits, Josiah started to say, but something in the trusting innocence of her face stopped him. That's when he was sure his discovery was correct. She believed everything he said.

There was never anyone who believed everything Josiah Hutchinson said, and he tested Rebecca every day.

One day she followed him into the woods to gather some kindling for the supper fire, and she said, "What's that, Joshua?"

"What?" he said absently.

"That blue."

"Blue what?"

He stood up straight and caught a fleeting glimpse of something blue disappearing into the woods. He wanted to call out, "Squaw!" He was beginning to wonder why, after all these years of rarely seeing an Indian inside the village, the old Indian woman seemed to be popping up wherever he was. Instead, he looked slyly at Rebecca.

"It was an Indian," he said.

Her eyes popped. "In—dian?"

"Aye."

"What was he doing?"

"Watching."

"Watching who?"

"Elizabeth."

"No!" Rebecca flung the doll behind her back and began to shake. "They can't have Elizabeth!"

"Then don't bring her into the woods," Josiah said simply.

He continued to gather kindling and was several yards from her before he realized she wasn't following. He looked up to find her frozen to the ground, clinging to Elizabeth and moaning.

"What's the matter?" he asked.

"If I can't bring Elizabeth, then I can't come." Her voice was thick with confusion.

"Well, that's easy," Josiah said. "Don't come."

"But Joshua!" she burst out. "I want—I want to be with *you*!"

For a long minute a pang shuddered through Josiah. She

did trust him—with that silly doll, with her life even, he thought. Maybe it wasn't a good idea to make up stories to scare her—

Josiah took a few steps toward her, and her face brightened as if she thought he was about to say something that would wipe away all her fear.

"All right, then," Josiah said. "Just keep her under your skirts when you come out in the woods and—she'll be safe."

The sun rose over Rebecca's face, and stuffing Elizabeth under her apron, she happily followed Josiah back to the farmhouse. Something began to nag at Josiah then, something he couldn't name, something he tried to brush away to the back of his mind.

"How is your cousin Rebecca, Captain?" Joseph Putnam asked a few days later when the four of them were out in the yard discussing the world. There weren't many warm days left, and he wanted to take advantage of the Indian summer, he said.

"Aye, she's fine," Josiah mumbled. *Could no one talk of anything else but her?*

"She's fine as long as she has 'Joshua'!" Ezekiel said.

Joseph looked at him carefully and then looked back at Josiah. "She likes you, does she?"

"Aye, I suppose." Josiah squirmed inside his vest.

"He loves her, too," Ezekiel said. "Perhaps it's because he has finally found someone even slower than he is!"

Joseph shot Ezekiel a dark look that seemed to bring even the birds to a freeze in the trees above them. Ezekiel's sharp-cheeked smile faded.

"I was only joking," he said timidly.

"Jokes are meant to be funny," Joseph said. "That wasn't."
He cleared his throat and folded his arms, and all three of
them sank low to the ground. Joseph Putnam didn't become
stern often, and when he did, it was deserved.

"To begin with," Joseph said, "Josiah is not slow. He thinks
before he speaks, and he thinks before he acts. A rare trait we
might all try to imitate, eh?" He looked darkly at William and
Ezekiel, but Josiah didn't feel at all good. "Now," he went on,
"it is obvious that young Rebecca is somewhat different—
somewhat, as you say, 'slower' than the rest of us, eh?"

Heads nodded.

"But let you remember this, gentlemen," he said. "There is
not a person walking this earth who has not been given some
gift by God that no one else has. Let you help Rebecca find
her gift, instead of poking fun at what she lacks."

He looked hard at Ezekiel and hard at William. For some
reason, Josiah wasn't surprised when he looked hard at him,
too.

Joseph gave them a few minutes to stew in that juice before
he clapped his hands and flashed them a smile. "Now, then,
enough of that. I have good news, and from the looks of those
faces, I think you could use some."

Josiah sat up in anticipation, and he heard Ezekiel and
William let out relieved sighs.

"As you know, I'm to be married in a few weeks, and since
the wedding is to be held in Salem Town and that requires a
good deal of travel—well, you already know that you boys won't
be attending the wedding." He leaned forward and whispered

loudly, "Dreadful boring things, weddings, anyway, eh?"

"Aye!" said Ezekiel.

"But since you gentlemen have been with me through my courtship of Mistress Constance Porter, you should have some share in the celebration of our marriage. I have arranged for a hayride for the young people of Salem Village some three days hence. What say you to that?"

A howling went up on Israel Porter's lawn that brought Constance herself to the front step to be sure no one was being murdered in the yard.

"All right, then," Joseph said, "let you spread the word among all the young people of the village. All are invited." As William and Ezekiel set to ticking off names on their fingers, Joseph leaned close to Josiah. "Rebecca is invited as well, Captain. I would like to see her there."

Josiah nodded dutifully. It might not be so bad. What could ruin a hayride?

✠ ⚜ ✠

apa always said there comes a day in every Massachusetts autumn when you know the trees are at their brightest. They have been building their colors since September, and on that one day, they will show off for the world with a brilliance that will hurt your eyes. And the next morning, you know that was the day, because the colors will begin to fade and wash away and the leaves will tumble to the ground in a mad flurry. You know very soon the trees will be naked and winter will be here. You'd better enjoy that day like no other, Papa always said.

As Josiah, Hope, and Rebecca walked to Israel Porter's the morning of Joseph Putnam's hayride, Josiah had a feeling today was the brightest day. The air fairly sizzled with the blaze of colors, and those same flames of gold and crimson flew all around him as the leaves pulled away from their branches and floated to freedom.

The air had just the right nip, too, the kind that made his skin tingle and his nose turn pink. He wore a leather vest while the girls had on short cloaks they could pull around them.

"Why must you two poke?" Hope said.

She was several steps ahead of him, and Rebecca was, as usual, trailing along behind.

"There will be plenty of room," Josiah told her. "Joseph said there will be two wagons."

"And would you prefer to sit in one full of Putnams?" Hope wanted to know.

"Putnams?"

"Aye. Joseph Putnam said all the village children were to be invited," she said. "Just as he invited them all to come to his school."

Josiah snickered. "You don't really suppose they'll come, do you?"

They rounded the bend in the Ipswich Road, and Hope stopped and pointed. "Does that answer your question?"

There ahead of them, hiking toward Israel Porter's, were a stream of young villagers. Jonathon Putnam led the way, followed by Eleazer and Richard and Ann Putnam, his sister. Silas Putnam, Edward's son, who was Hope's age, was among them, too, and Abigail Williams, Reverend Parris's niece. Only the minister's daughter, Betty Parris, was missing. She was said to be sickly, and she rarely came out when there was the slightest chill in the air.

Abigail was the first to see Hope, and she turned and whispered to the others. Almost like one person they turned to give a big-headed, red-faced Putnam stare.

Rebecca stopped dead in her tracks. "Bandits!" she whispered.

"They won't hurt you today," Josiah said quickly.

"Why?" she asked.

"Because—too many people. Come on."

"What did she say?" Hope said.

"Nothing."

Hope took hold of Rebecca's arm and began to run. "Now we really have to hurry if we don't want to sit with all of them."

They ran across Israel Porter's yard, dragging Rebecca along between them, and careened down the hill toward the barn where the wagons would be hitched up and piled high with hay. Josiah could smell its sweet odor already.

"No! Oh, no, Joshua!"

Rebecca halted abruptly, nearly throwing both Hope and Josiah to the ground. They had the wagons in sight now, and the Proctors and the Porters stood within earshot, staring up at them.

"What's the matter now?" Hope said peevishly. "What is it?"

Rebecca shook her head slowly. Her face was white, and she pointed at the oxen that were hitched up to the wagons.

"Oxen, Joshua!" she cried.

"So?" Hope squinted impatiently at Josiah. "What is she talking about?"

Josiah shrugged guiltily.

"They're just cattle, Rebecca," Hope said. "They won't hurt you."

"Aye—they will. They'll eat me—Joshua said—"

Josiah snatched her arm and took off with her toward the wagons. "Only if they don't get enough hay. And see? There's plenty of hay. Now shut it!"

"Josiah!" Hope called as she chased after them. "What is she talking about?"

When they got to the barn, Josiah let go of her hand and slithered between Rachel Porter and Sarah Proctor to get to William and Ezekiel. He didn't wait to see where Rebecca went.

"You beat the Putnams here, eh?" William said.

"Aye." Josiah leaned over to catch his breath. "They're all comin' over the hill soon. We saw them on the road." Josiah looked at Ezekiel, who hadn't said a word yet but was carefully studying a piece of straw. "Which wagon are we riding in?"

"*I* am going in whichever wagon *she* isn't going in." Ezekiel pointed the straw toward the wagons. Josiah followed it with his eyes, and saw Rebecca carrying an armful of hay from the barn as fast as her chunky legs would go and dropping it under the noses of the uninterested oxen—and then tearing back toward the barn.

"What is she *doing*?" Rachel said.

"She thinks the oxen are going to eat her or something," Hope said. "I suppose she's making sure they aren't hungry."

"Why does she think that?" asked Sarah.

Ezekiel snickered. "Because that's her gift." He poked William in the side, and William chuckled halfheartedly.

"All right, then—shall we begin?" called a voice from around the side of the barn. Smiling his big, fresh smile, Joseph Putnam appeared and the children thronged around him. Josiah stayed at the back of the crowd and pulled Rebecca roughly over to him.

"They aren't hungry anymore," he whispered harshly.

She nodded solemnly and hugged Elizabeth to her. *Probably to protect the thing from bandits and Indians,* Josiah thought. Why hadn't he told her hayrides were danger-ous for ten-year-old girls?

By then Joseph had given the okay, and the children raced toward the two wagons. Still dragging Rebecca behind him, Josiah slid through the crowd and found Ezekiel. But when he put his foot up on the wheel to follow him, Ezekiel turned around and said, "I told you I'm not riding with—" He nodded toward Rebecca.

Josiah stared at him blankly. Around him, the other chil-dren piled into the wagon, but still Ezekiel shook his head.

"I have a right to ride in this wagon, Ezekiel Porter!" Josiah said.

"Good, then—I'll ride in another." Ezekiel slung his leg over the side, but Rachel clutched his arm.

"Papa said we're not to ride with any of the Putnams," she said. "And that's all that's in that wagon."

Ezekiel shrugged and pulled his leg back in. Still, Josiah stared.

"Captain!" Joseph Putnam called. "Will you and your family be coming aboard today?"

"Come on, Hope!" Sarah Proctor cried in her high-pitched voice. She stuck an arm out to Hope, and Hope grabbed hold.

"Choose a wagon and climb on, Captain!" Joseph strode

toward Josiah and looked up, puzzled. "What's the trouble? Why don't you get aboard?"

Josiah looked from Joseph to the top of the wagon.

"Come on, Josiah!" Hope called down.

She was grabbed from behind by Rachel Porter. Josiah waited.

"Can we get in now?" Rebecca said loudly.

"I don't see why not!" Joseph Putnam reached down to pick up Rebecca, when suddenly Hope flung herself from the wagon and landed on the ground beside him.

"We'll ride in the other wagon," she said tightly. "Come Rebecca, Josiah."

She took Rebecca's hand from Joseph and marched stiffly to the other wagon. Josiah looked up at Ezekiel and William, but neither of them would look at him.

"You're riding in the other wagon?" Joseph Putnam asked.

"I suppose," Josiah said.

Even as Joseph Putnam looked sternly up at his other two students, Josiah stepped past him to the second wagon where Hope and Rebecca were climbing in. Its passengers crowded to the other side as if the newcomers were bringing a dreaded disease on board. When Josiah appeared, a roar went up.

"Th—th—this wagon is f—f—full!" Jonathon said, his lip curled.

"W—w—well—at l—l—least he didn't bring his Indian squ—squ—squaw!" Eleazer shrieked.

Josiah ignored them and sank into the hay beside Hope. Rebecca wriggled in happily on his other side and put her head on his shoulder. He squirmed away and stared at the toes of his boots.

"Good, then—if we're all in tight—off we go!" Joseph Putnam shouted. "I shall see you at Solomon's Hill!"

He backed away from the wagons, and Giles Porter hopped up onto the seat of Josiah's wagon and clucked at the oxen. In spite of the pleasant rocking and the sweet smell of the hay and the baskets of apples and wild pears and nuts that dotted their straw mattress, Josiah wished he had never come. He had to take care of Rebecca—his father had made that plain. But she was bothersome to be around with her loud voice and constant questions and drooping mouth. His friends wouldn't be with her, and that meant they wouldn't be with him. He gnawed savagely at his lip.

From Israel Porter's to Goff's Bridge, the Putnams stared at the Hutchinsons with glittering eyes. But when Hope only stared back, the Putnams and Abigail formed a tight circle and whispered amongst themselves.

Rebecca cowered behind Josiah's shoulder. "Are they planning?" she whispered.

"Yes," Josiah whispered back. "And they don't like people talking while they're planning."

Rebecca clapped both hands over her mouth and sank down in the hay.

Hope narrowed her eyes at Josiah. "What kinds of things are you telling her?"

"Nothing." Josiah plunked his chin down on his knees, which he had hitched up in front of him.

"Don't let them think you aren't having fun," Hope whispered.

"We have a right to have fun, same as they do."

Josiah put his mouth close to her ear. "You could have stayed in that other wagon. It was Rebecca they didn't want."

"Ha!" Hope said.

Jonathon and Eleazer twisted their big heads toward her and she smiled sweetly. They turned away.

"I wasn't going to let you ride in here with these animals by yourself!" she hissed.

"I can take care of myself."

"Well besides, I don't want to be with people who are mean."

"Like Ezekiel?"

"Aye—and Rachel. And William and Sarah go along with whatever they say. They're spineless! If they can't accept my cousin, then I don't want to be with them."

Josiah snuck a peek at Rebecca. She had her head buried in the hay. "I thought she made you crazy," he said to Hope.

"She does. But she's our family. We can't just let people be cruel to her."

Nagging thoughts began to tug at the back of Josiah's brain. He brushed them away by changing the subject.

"But they're your friends," Josiah said to Hope.

She shrugged. "Sarah and Rachel aren't the only friends a person can have."

"Who else is there?"

Hope cocked her head in thought, and her eyes slanted toward the Putnams. "I don't know. I'll find someone."

"Not them! Papa would—"

"Papa can choose his friends and I can choose mine!" she snapped.

And with that she sank into a cold silence.

Josiah didn't think he had ever felt lonelier.

And so although a party was waiting for them at the bottom of Solomon's Hill—with pies and tarts and chocolate and Josiah's favorite macaroons—and with games and stories and a pair of fiddlers—it was the most miserable day Josiah had spent in his 11 years.

Hope paired up with Abigail in one of the games, and when next Josiah looked for her, the two of them were huddled beneath a poplar, laughing and whispering and pointing the way girls always did.

Rebecca followed him everywhere, which brought cackling and sneering from the Putnams, and stony silence from Ezekiel and William. The only good part of the day was that Rebecca didn't ask any questions. She kept her eyes on Jonathon Putnam and her hands clapped firmly over her mouth.

Joseph Putnam came around several times, but each time he had the pretty, blushing Constance, his bride, on his arm. Josiah could never think of anything to say around her.

"How is my lovely Rebecca today?" Joseph said on one visit.

"Shh!" she said, her eyes swelling. "The ban-dits are planning!"

Joseph looked puzzled, and his eyes went to Josiah.

"That sounds like a fun game!" Constance said.

"Aye, it is," Josiah said miserably.

But as Joseph looked back over his shoulder as they walked on, Josiah knew he didn't believe him.

"Come on, Rebecca," Josiah said suddenly. "We are walking home."

"Why?" she said—of course.

"We want to stay away from the bandits," he said.

✝ ✦ ✝

Chapter Eight

Two angry, silent bodies lay on their beds in their room that night. The air was thick with their raging thoughts.

Hope lay stiff as a post as she fumed, but Josiah flopped back and forth like a flounder. Hope finally yanked aside her bed curtains and said, "Would you please be quiet?"

"No." And Josiah gave another noisy flip to the side of his cot.

"Ach!" Hope flounced from the bed and pranced to the window. "There is no point in trying to sleep here."

Josiah sat up and wiggled his shoulders. He was used to Hope being angry with him. He wasn't used to being angry with her, and he wasn't sure what to do or say. He grabbed at the first bitter thought.

"Why did you spend the whole day with Abigail Williams?" he asked.

"That is purely my business." She tossed her black curls off her shoulders.

"It's my business, too, when it means I have to spend my whole day with—her."

"I shall be friends with whomever I choose, Joseph Hutchinson!" she said.

"I'm Josiah!"

"I know." She gave him a dark look over her shoulder and then tossed her head back toward the window. Josiah slipped from his cot and joined her.

"You want to be friends with Abigail just to make Papa angry?" he said. "I don't understand—"

"It isn't to make Papa angry. I do that just by walking into the room, it seems. I'm doing it to show him that he cannot rule what I think and what I want and whom I want to spend my time with!"

"But Abigail Williams did a terrible thing to you last summer! Why would you want to be friends with her?"

"I've forgiven her," Hope said stubbornly. "Christians are supposed to forgive."

Josiah opened his mouth to answer, but then he heard it. A wolf—one wolf—was howling, and close. Was it their wolf— the one with the thick, beautiful tail? He fumbled with the window and opened it.

"It's cold, Josiah!" Hope said.

"I want to hear the wolves!"

"Aaaaah! Between you with the wolves and Rebecca with the oxen and the bandits—"

"Me?" said a dull, too-loud voice through a crack in the

door. "Rebecca—me?"

"Who else?" Hope dove into her bed and snapped the curtains closed behind her.

At the window, Josiah groaned inwardly. Rebecca padded, happily and noisily, to his side.

"Why are you awake, Rebecca?" he asked.

She looked at him blankly, mouth drooping. She wasn't used to being asked the questions, and it took her a while to answer. Josiah drummed his fingers on the top of the trunk.

"I heard something," she said finally.

"You heard us talking. Go back to bed."

"No," she said, slowly shaking her head. "No."

"What was it, then?"

She considered that for a moment. "It sounded like this." Pursing her lips into a kiss, she put her head back and softly howled.

Josiah stared. She sounded just like the wolves—his wolves. Even Hope whipped back the bed curtains and ran her eyes around the room before clapping them back together again and disappearing.

"What is that sound, Joshua?" Rebecca said. "Have you ever heard it before?"

Her pale eyes were round with wonder and fear, and for a moment Josiah felt something strange. He suddenly wanted to protect her, to take the fear from her face and replace it with the comfort that "Joshua" was there.

But then another feeling crept in—the one he felt more than any other lately. The feeling that the presence of this plodding little girl at his side all the time was taking away everything good and fun in his life. If he protected Rebecca, he couldn't have Ezekiel or William—or even Hope. He was the butt of every joke in the Putnam clan, and he couldn't even sit here in his window alone and figure out what to do about it. She was always there, always asking questions, always afraid, always clutching at his hand—

"They're Indians, Rebecca!" he burst out.

Her stubby hands went to her cheeks, and everything on her face widened. "In-dians?" she said breathlessly.

"Aye. They howl so you'll think they're wolves."

"Why?"

"Because—they're children of the devil." Josiah had actually heard Reverend Parris say that. At the time he had thought of Oneko and decided that perhaps Reverend Parris knew different Indians than he did. But just as always, Rebecca believed it because it came out of "Joshua's" mouth.

"Will—will they get us, Joshua?" she said in a hoarse whisper they probably heard in Topsfield.

"Oh, probably not. But maybe."

"Oh!"

"But don't worry, Rebecca." Josiah felt something sly about to come out of his mouth. Something a little bit frightening, maybe a little bit cruel. "You will know if they're about to come after you."

If it were possible, her eyes doubled in size. "How will I know?"

"They will leave a sign on the door."

"What kind of sign?"

Josiah floundered for a minute. He had heard that the

Indians left warning signs, but he had no idea what they were. And he was pretty sure no one in Salem Village had ever seen one on their house. He dug into his imagination.

"Maybe a tomahawk stuck in the clapboards," Josiah said. "Or the tail of some animal. Every tribe is different," he finished lamely.

The hands on the sides of Rebecca's chubby face began to shake. "What—what should I do if I see a sign?" she asked in a wobbly voice.

"Why, run, of course!"

He knew her next question would be "where shall I run?" and he was trying to find a creative answer in the darkest corners of the mean part of his mind, when she surprised him.

"I know just where I'll run," she said.

Josiah stared at her. "Where?"

"I'll run straight to God." She nodded her head slowly. "I'll run straight to God."

With those five words, all the sport went out of the game. Even the most twisted kind of fun he'd had drained out of Josiah. He was left with only the nagging voices at the back of his brain, and they were louder than ever.

"I must go back to my mama now," Rebecca said. "Will you be all right, Joshua?"

"Aye," Josiah said quietly. "I'll be fine."

But as she padded heavily back to the sitting room, Josiah wasn't really quite sure.

It appeared in the weeks following the hayride that the Putnam boys had nothing better to do with their time in the late afternoons than to wait for Josiah to leave Israel Porter's so they could badger him on his way home. No matter which way he went, they were there.

If he went straight across Ipswich Road and past Nathaniel Putnam's, they hid in the orchard and threw the last of the rotting apples that lay on the ground at him, taunting, "Oh, Joshu-a, Joshu-a! Save me from the ban-dits!"

If he went far north and came down Thorndike Hill, they were waiting to ambush him at the bottom with pouches full of nuts that they slung at him, chanting, "Joshu-a, Joshu-a! The oxen will eat me!" or "I'm glad you don't have your squaw with you, Joshua. I'm so afraid of her!"

Every time, Josiah stayed calm on the outside and pretended they didn't scare him. He talked carefully and found ways to divert their attention so they would start fighting among themselves, and he could slip away. Each time he thought he'd proven that he was not a brainless boy or a stuttering idiot. But the next day, they wanted *the proof* all over again. It occurred to Josiah one day that if he could start proving what he *was* instead of what he *wasn't*, they might leave him alone. But he didn't know the answer to who he was. He only knew he was tired of the game.

Sometimes he lingered at school long after William and Ezekiel were gone, hoping the Putnams would get tired of waiting and go home. One afternoon as he dawdled in putting away his books, he caught Joseph Putnam watching him from the doorway. When Josiah crossed the room to leave, Joseph blocked his way.

"You have something on your mind, Captain," he said.

"But, of course, you've got it well in hand, so I needn't offer my help."

One look at Josiah's face told him he didn't, and Josiah knew it. He hung his head.

"Captain!" Joseph pulled Josiah's chin up with his hand. "I haven't seen you do that in months. I thought we had that all settled last summer, eh?"

"Aye." Josiah wagged his head. "But this time—"

Joseph took Josiah by the elbow. "Come with me."

He led Josiah down the hall to the back of Israel Porter's big house and into the kitchen. It was quiet for the moment, with no one bustling about and only a small fire crackling in the fireplace to ward off the autumn chill. Joseph went to a cupboard and pulled out a plate covered with a white linen napkin. He set it on the table, motioned for Josiah to sit, and swept the cover off. The plate was piled high with macaroons.

"I noticed you didn't have much of an appetite at the hayride the other day," Joseph said. "I thought you might like to make up for it now."

Josiah couldn't help grinning as he helped himself to a macaroon.

"Oh, come now." Joseph flashed one of his famous smiles. "You need at least one for each hand. Who knows when we'll be chased out of here? You don't want to have to leave empty-handed."

Shyly, Josiah selected a second one and took a bite. It *was* delicious, and he hadn't had one since last summer. The memory of that special time flooded back with the sweet flavor as he chewed.

"Now, let me tell you how I sometimes look at life," Joseph Putnam said, his own mouth bulging. "You do want to hear that, don't you, Captain?"

Josiah nodded, grinning through the crumbs.

"Life is like taking a ship out to sea. Sometimes the waters are calm, with just enough wind to carry you along—and you, Captain Josiah Hutchinson, are in control on the quarter-deck—the master of the ocean, eh?"

"I suppose," Josiah said.

"But every now and then, a storm comes up. You remember that storm last summer?"

"Aye."

"You can't foresee it. You can't stop it. You can only ride it out."

"Well, there *are* things you can do to save your ship," Josiah said.

"Aye, and you would know that—because it's your ship."

"Aye."

"Now—" Joseph Putnam leaned back and folded his hands, putting his fingers like a pistol under his chin as Josiah had seen him do before when he was about to say something to make Josiah think. "Is it true that once you've been through one storm, there will never be another?"

"No!"

"Is it true that you handle every storm the same way?"

"I don't think so."

"Is it true that as Captain you will always know how to handle your ship in every storm?"

"I should," Josiah said slowly.

"But what if you don't? What if you have done everything you know to do, and you still make mistakes—and the ship is about to sink!"

Joseph loved a story, and he leaned forward now, his face glowing close to Josiah's.

"You should pray," Josiah said. "I learned that last summer. Even when you've made a terrible mistake, you can still go to God. Then you learn what's right—and you never make that mistake again."

Joseph Putnam's eyebrows shot up. "Wrong."

Josiah stared. "Wrong?"

"Aye. There isn't a ship's captain alive—or any other person, for that matter—who hasn't made the same mistake a dozen times—or new mistakes. We are only human beings. That's why we need God—because we are always making mistakes. He doesn't care how many times we have to go to Him, because He knows that as we grow, we learn things—and we also figure out new ways to do the wrong thing."

He leaned back and munched thoughtfully on a macaroon. Josiah laid his on the table, and the part that was in his mouth turned to mud. He swallowed hard.

"I still have to prove to people all the time that I am not dumb," he said. "And when she came along, it was fun to make someone else feel dumb—for a while. But now it doesn't help anymore—and everything is still ruined."

"It isn't ruined, Captain," Joseph said softly. "It's only run aground for the moment. You and God will figure it out. I have faith in you."

"I have faith in you." Those words carried Josiah across Israel Porter's yard, past the nearly naked trees, and through the piles of leaves that crackled happily under his boots. For a few minutes, he had hope. Maybe he could be nicer to Rebecca. Maybe he could talk Hope out of being friends with Abigail. Maybe he could wait out the Putnams, and they'd get tired of him.

But his hope faded the minute he saw the Putnams coming up the Ipswich Road—looking for more *proof*.

✢ ✢ ✢

Chapter Nine

The Putnams were still far enough away that if he ducked through the marsh and ran south, they would pass him and he could then cross the Crane Bridge by his father's sawmill and run home. The marshes were at their driest this time of year, and if he was careful, he would only get a little muddy.

He remembered what Joseph Putnam had just said, and he prayed all the way. It seemed as if God did some pretty fast work then, for by the time he reached the Crane River, the Putnams were nowhere in sight. He sighed with relief and flopped down on the bank. He picked up a handful of pebbles and had only skipped a few across the glassy surface of the water when he heard the voices.

"He's there—he's down river!" he heard Eleazer Putnam say in a hoarse whisper that was no quieter than one of Rebecca's.

"Shh!" someone hissed. It could only have been Jonathon.

Wildly, Josiah looked around for an escape route. The only way to go was south, farther away from them—and farther away from home. He flattened to his belly and began to crawl in the brush by the water when he heard still another voice. This one whispered, "Boy!"

Josiah tried to perk his ears up to listen.

"Boy!" it said again.

"Squaw?" he whispered back.

For answer, he saw a bright blue shawl and a wide face that crackled a smile from the other side of the river. She raised her shoulders just high enough for him to see where she pointed. She was nodding for him to go upriver—toward where the Putnams were hissing and whispering to each other.

Josiah shook his head, but she bobbed hers and beckoned for him to come to her. Across the river.

Unlike most Puritans, Josiah had spent some time in the water. The rules of the church made it unlawful for a Puritan to put his entire body into the water, but Oneko, the Indian boy, had taken Josiah swimming in rougher, deeper water than this.

Still, Josiah shook his head. He had almost drowned in the Ipswich River once. Oneko, had saved him.

The voices of the Putmans grew closer.

"Boy!" the squaw whispered again.

She was halfway into the river herself, her head bare now and her skirts wallowing in the water. Even there, she was only in up to her knees. Softly, she beckoned to him again. Josiah quickly pulled off his boots, held them above the surface of the water, and plunged in.

Trying not to make any splashing noises, he made his way to the center where the squaw took his hand and pulled him safely to the other side. Just as she shoved him into the bushes, the Putnams popped up on the opposite bank.

"There are footprints here! He was here!" Josiah heard Richard say.

"He thinks himself a great scout!" Josiah whispered to the squaw.

She grabbed him by the arm then and pulled him noiselessly up the river, pressing one hand on the back of his neck to keep his head below the underbrush. The Putnams' voices faded behind him as they made their way. When they reached the Crane Bridge, just south of the sawmill, she smiled, pointed down river, and shook her head.

Josiah grinned and shook his, too. "They'll never find me now. Thank you."

Her sunrise face beamed and she patted his hand. She was warm now after their chase up the riverbank, and she pulled the blue shawl off her shoulder for a moment. Josiah looked at her, and he thought he saw something familiar dangling around her neck.

But she quickly pulled the shawl back around her and pointed down the river and across. Josiah craned to look. "Where are they now?" he whispered.

She didn't answer. When he looked, his squaw was gone.

Who is she, anyway? Josiah wondered. *Why is she always there?* He smiled to himself. *If she's going to keep saving me, she needs a name. I think I'll call her—Wife of Wolf—*

But before he could roll the words around in his brain and get used to the sound of them, he heard voices again. This time they rumbled angrily from the direction of the sawmill and then stopped directly over his head on the bridge.

"Thomas Putnam, how many times must I tell you that I will not be a part of your little militia against the Indians?" said one firm but quiet voice. It was Josiah's father.

"You'll be sorry, then, Hutchinson!" cried Thomas Putnam. Josiah could almost imagine his big face glowing red. "You'll be sorry the first time those savages burn your house or kill one of your children."

"Good heavens, Putnam," Joseph Hutchinson said wearily. "We have no 'savages' living near Salem Village."

"What do you call those brown-faced devils selling their baskets within spitting distance of this very mill?"

"Do you really equate those Indians with 'savages'? They are selling baskets, as you say."

"And scouting at the same time!"

Josiah's father laughed.

"Laugh at me if you want, Hutchinson! You know your history, do you not?"

"I surely do," Papa said calmly.

Beneath the bridge, Josiah rolled his eyes. Everyone knew his father was the village expert on Massachusetts history. The Putnams themselves had criticized him for spending as much time reading history books as he did reading the Bible.

"Then, you know about the King Phillip War," Thomas Putnam raged on, "and the uprisings in Maine that are going on right now. Why, our men must now go into Quebec—"

"You know just enough to make you dangerous, Mr. Putnam," Josiah's father said in his quiet voice that hammered like a silent mallet. "The Indians were savage in the King Phillip War because they were persuaded that to fight with the king was the right thing to do—and do you know how they ended up?"

"Well, I—"

"Hundreds of Indians were sold into slavery—and those who weren't were executed. That war led to the almost total destruction of the southern New England Indian nations—wiped out the strength of the Wampanoags, the Narragansets, the Nipmucks."

"Good riddance, then!" Thomas Putnam cried.

Papa's voice was quiet. "Do you know what our early settlers called those Indians, Mr. Putnam?"

"Nay, but—"

"Praying Indians," Papa said.

There was silence on the bridge, and Josiah almost had to stop breathing to keep from being detected. Finally, Thomas Putnam cleared his throat.

"I do not see what any of that has to do with our protecting ourselves from the Indians here," he said gruffly.

"Neither do I," Papa said. "We have at least an unspoken agreement with the Indians near our village to leave each other alone. Why should we prepare ourselves against an attack that is never going to come?"

"Now see here—"

"Putnam! Isn't that—is that not your boy, Richard, I see crawling up the riverbank there?"

"What—have you gone mad, Hutchinson?" Thomas sputtered.

But Josiah heard his boots clunking across the bridge, and then he heard him gasp over the railing.

"Richard!" Thomas Putnam cried. "Is it you, indeed?"

There was more clunking as Thomas left the bridge and took to the riverbank. From his vantage point on the other side, Josiah saw Thomas traipsing through the underbrush in his fine waistcoat, pawing the air with his sleeves in anger. Josiah covered his mouth to keep from laughing.

Above him, his father chuckled softly. "Poor pitiful man," Josiah heard him say.

It was almost dark when Josiah decided it was safe to come out from under the bridge. His father had long since returned to the mill, and Thomas Putnam had dragged his son Richard off by the ear, calling back to his nephews to go home where they belonged.

They hadn't followed those instructions right away, however, and Josiah had stayed crouched amid the cattails while they searched the brush on the other side of the river trying to find him. Only when Ann appeared on horseback to tell them that Uncle Nathaniel was about to come looking for Jonathon did they give up the search. *Those Putnams certainly stick together,* Josiah thought.

This thought stayed with him all the way home. What about the Hutchinsons? Did they stay together? What about Hope, going off to make friends with Abigail Williams just because she was angry with her father? What about Josiah frightening his own cousin, just because he could? It was time, he decided, to do something about all that. He wasn't sure what yet—but it was time.

The opportunity didn't present itself that night. He had chores to do when he got home. Then it was time for supper. And his father chose that night to have him read the Bible aloud for the family so his Aunt Esther could see how far he had come in his studies.

She nodded while he read, and she told him softly when he was finished that she thought him a "fine boy." But then her thoughts seemed to drift off as always, and she lost herself in her knitting.

Josiah hadn't gotten to know Aunt Esther well since she'd come to stay with them. She was often busy with Mama and Hope—and often she seemed to be somewhere else. Mama had whispered to him and Hope that she was grieving, and not to ask her too many questions. He was pretty sure that was mostly for Hope's benefit. He didn't usually have much to say around grown-ups.

But tonight, someone else in the room was obviously impressed with his reading. When he put the family's Geneva Bible back into its box, he noticed Rebecca crouched by the fire with Elizabeth on her lap, gazing at him with wide, shining eyes. As the light of the flames played across her face, so did the obvious admiration.

When she saw him looking back at her, she fumbled for words. "Joshua—" she said in her too-loud way, "you are the smartest boy—I ever knew."

"Now that's saying something," Hope muttered as he passed her. "It's certain *she* knows smart when she sees it."

Josiah didn't smile. The nagging thoughts screamed at him now, and he could not smile.

✢ ✢ ✢

Chapter Ten

osiah thought it was the howling of the wolves that awakened him the next morning, and he fought his way out of sleep thinking, *They don't usually howl in the morning. Why are they crying now when the sun's coming up?*

But when he sat up on his cot, fully awake, he knew it wasn't howling at all—at least not from the wolves. Someone was crying in loud, piteous sobs.

Hope heard it, too, and she stood with her ear pressed against the door of their room.

"Who is that?" Josiah asked.

"I don't know—I can't hear. Can you listen?"

Josiah crept from his bed and tiptoed to the door, although the crying was now so loud, no one would hear him if he stomped across the room.

Josiah put his ear to the door. On the other side, Aunt

Esther sobbed, and his mother spoke in a quiet stream of words.

"You've naught to be frightened over, Esther," Mama was saying. "You and Daniel are not the cause."

"What are they saying?" Hope said.

Josiah waved her off and listened.

"They know I'm here! The Indians know I'm here!" Aunt Esther cried. Her voice seemed to be teetering on the edge of some dangerous cliff. "I am the wife of a man who fought against their own, and they know I'm here! I must leave, Deborah! I must leave at once!"

"No!" Mama said in as loud a voice as Josiah had ever heard her use. Even Hope's face jumped in concern.

There was a scuffling noise on the other side of the door, and Mama cried out, "Joseph! Joseph, come help me!"

Josiah threw open the door in time to see Aunt Esther pulling away from Mama and trying to get to the top of the stairs. Her eyes were wild—like the wolf's they'd cornered in the woods—and Josiah stood frozen to the floor as he watched her.

"Josiah, help me hold her!" Mama cried.

Hope shoved him from behind, and both of them grabbed Aunt Esther's arms and dragged her back toward the bed. Mama kept calling Papa's name, and finally they heard his boots on the steps and he lumbered into the tiny room.

Within minutes he had his sister pinned to her bed, and although she was breathing hard, her eyes were fastened on him and she was listening.

"Esther, this has naught to do with you!" he said into her face.

Next to him, Hope squeezed Josiah's hand to get his attention. When he looked at her, her eyes were quizzical. Josiah shrugged. He had no idea what they were talking about.

"I have no notion whether it is truly an Indian warning sign," Papa said. "You say Rebecca called it that when she saw it, but Esther, she is only a child—what does she know of such things?"

"Perhaps she heard of it in Maine. She has cause enough to be frightened of the Indians, Joseph. They killed her father!"

Something inside Josiah gave way—and a hundred screaming voices clawed at the back of his brain.

Aunt Esther started to sob again, and Mama held her in her arms and rocked her. Papa put one of his big, rough hands on her head.

"Even so, we have no reason to think that the Indians here would do such a thing. Josiah and Hope even had one as a friend."

"Unless they know I am here," Esther said stubbornly.

"Or unless this is not the work of Indians at all." The deadly calm in Papa's voice brought everyone's gaze up to meet his.

No one asked a question, though, for Papa suddenly straightened and headed for the stairs. Josiah and Hope backed away.

"Children," Papa said, "get you dressed and come downstairs. There are chores to do, and—I have something to show you."

"Hope," Mama said. "I think some comfrey root tea would be good for Aunt Esther, eh?"

"Aye," Hope said softly.

Comfrey root tea was a remedy they'd learned from the widow, who herself had learned it from her Indian friends. It was made to calm an upset person and put her to sleep. Aunt Esther was certainly in need of that.

"I must get up and help you, Deborah," Aunt Esther said as Hope and Josiah hurried into their room.

"You'll do nothing but rest in this bed and let God gather your wits for you," Mama said.

In the kitchen, Papa stood with his back to them, seeming to stare into the fire. But when they came in, he turned to face them, and in his hands he held something gray and furry.

Hope put her hand to her mouth. "Papa! Is that—is that a wolf's tail?"

Josiah nearly shoved her out of the way to see. As Papa held it out to them, he was sure of it. It was thick and shiny and every shade of gray. A leather strap was wrapped around its top, and from it dangled several feathers. It was the same tail they'd seen on the wolf they'd run off in the wolf rout—Josiah knew it.

"Your cousin Rebecca was up early this morning," Papa said. "Apparently she has bad dreams some nights and tries to run from the house. When she fled out the front door before dawn, she found this hanging there." Papa's eyes pierced through them. "Do either of you have any idea where it may have come from?"

Josiah immediately shook his head, but his thoughts were chasing each other wildly through his brain. *I told her the*

Indians would leave a sign if they were after her. I told her it might be an animal's tail. But I didn't even know that could be a real sign. I didn't know—and I didn't do it! I was going to tell her it was all a foolish joke—

"Josiah!" Papa said sharply. "You look as if you are ill. Tell me—do you know anything about where this might have come from?"

"No, sir," Josiah said. That was true—and the truth frightened him.

"Hope?" Papa said.

"No, sir," she answered.

Josiah looked at her quickly out of the corner of his eye. She had been quiet since the scene upstairs, and now she was quieter still. He was sure she knew nothing because, although Hope might be sullen and rebellious at times, she never lied.

Papa sighed and tossed the wolf's tail onto the table in disgust. "This is an act of pure cruelty," he said, "and I've a mind to discover who has done such a thing. In the meantime, your mother will be busy caring for Aunt Esther. This is a great setback for her in her grief. I must count on you, Hope, to take care of things here, and you, Josiah, to watch out for your cousin. She seems to have taken a liking to you. Perhaps you can help her most."

Papa left the kitchen, and Hope went straight to the fire to prepare breakfast. Josiah stood still as a statue in the middle of the room.

Watch out for your cousin, Papa had said.

He would watch out for her—*but where was she?*

With a sickening feeling of dread, Josiah made for the

door. *If you should see such a sign,* he had told Rebecca in the dark of one horrible night, *run away.*

What if, indeed, she had done just that?

Josiah had barely gotten across the yard when Hope called to him from the front door. He kept going, and she had to run to catch up to him.

"Josiah, where are you going?" she asked.

He stopped. Of course, he didn't know.

"I have to tell you something," she said.

Something about the way she put her hand on his arm made him look at her closely. Her black eyes were glazed with fear.

"I think I know how that wolf's tail got on our door," she said.

"It wasn't my fault—" Josiah started to say, but Hope went on.

"I was with Abigail late yesterday, just before you came home. I promised I'd meet her when I went to fetch water." Hope looked over both shoulders and leaned close to Josiah's ear. Her voice touched it in frosty puffs. "She told me that she saw John Indian talking to Thomas Putnam just before."

"Who's John Indian?"

"He's one of Reverend Parris's slaves—he brought him here from Barbados when he was a merchant there. He isn't one of *our* Indians—that's just his name."

"But how does that—"

"Abigail sneaked over to listen to them, and she said she only caught part of the conversation, but what she did hear was that Thomas Putnam was paying John Indian to play some kind of trick on someone in the village."

"Why did she tell you?"

"She said she was sure it was Papa he was playing the trick on. Who else would it be?"

Josiah felt his eyes growing wide. "Abigail Williams was warning *us*?"

Hope looked down and toyed with the hem of her apron. "Not exactly," she said. "I told her at the hayride that I was mad at Papa—so she thought I would be—happy—to hear that Papa was going to be the butt of some joke."

Josiah's mouth dropped open, but just as quickly he closed it. Who was he to point his finger at Hope when he was guilty of a much worse crime?

"You must think I'm a wicked wretch," she said, still staring down at her apron.

"No worse than I am," he said.

"Oh?"

Looking down at his boots, Josiah told her. The words almost refused to come—he had to squeeze them out like chickens squirming under a fence. When he was finished, he was afraid to look up.

"Well, then," Hope said, clapping her hands.

"What?"

"Perhaps Reverend Parris is right. Maybe we are just evil children. But we can cry over that later, Josiah. Right now, we must make things right. I must go to Abigail and find out what more I can—and then Papa has to be told."

"Are you afraid?" Josiah asked.

"I'm more afraid of Abigail. You—you must find Rebecca."

Josiah's heart jumped. "Aye!"

"Do you have any idea where she might be?"

Actually, Josiah had at least a dozen, but before he could start on any of them, there was something he needed. If he told Rebecca that her idol "Joshua" was a liar, she would need another friend she could trust to take his place.

＋ ⸱＋⸱ ＋

$\mathcal{A}$ unt Esther was sleeping and Mama was down in the herb garden gathering more comfrey root when Josiah slipped into the sitting room and peered through the semidarkness. The shutters were closed to allow Aunt Esther to rest—which she didn't seem to be doing as far as Josiah could see. Her eyes were closed and she slept, but her fingers were fidgety on the bedcovers, and she let out a little cry with every breath.

For a minute Josiah watched her. He had never seen anyone grieve before. He was sad when he lost the widow, but this grief looked like pain. He hoped it was something he never had to feel. And if Aunt Esther lost anything else—he would be responsible.

He shook himself and peered again around the room. There on the pillow next to Aunt Esther was what he was looking for. He knew it would be here. Ever since he told

Rebecca practically every group in Salem Village was after Elizabeth, she'd forced herself to leave her behind.

Slowing down his every move, he leaned over and picked up the doll. As soon as he had it in his hand, Aunt Esther's eyes fluttered open.

"Oh!" she cried out. With terror in her eyes, she struggled to sit up.

"No, Aunt Esther!" Josiah whispered. "Go back to sleep! I—" He looked at the doll in his hand. "Rebecca just wants Elizabeth."

Slowly, the fear faded from her face and she lay back down on the cushions. "Thank you, Josiah. You are so kind to my daughter. Take care of her while I rest, would you?"

"I will," he said. And a million nagging voices screamed in his head.

The first problem, of course, was that he was supposed to be in school with Joseph Putnam. If Joseph saw his father during the day, he would ask where Josiah was. He shook that thought away. He would find Rebecca almost before it was time to be in school and would barely miss a thing. And if he did, Joseph Putnam, he knew, would understand. It was another way to get his ship through the storm. And Papa?

Josiah shook that thought away, too, and began to run.

His first stop was the orchard, where Rebecca loved to go because she thought she was helping "Joshua." It took twice as long to get there as usual, for he was trying to stay out of sight in case any of the other villagers should see him and report his running about to his father before he could find her.

But she wasn't in the orchard; nor was she in the barn, or the pastures, or the fields. The sun was rising higher in the sky. Joseph Putnam would be drilling William and Ezekiel in their arithmetic and glancing out the window every now and then to look for him. Josiah leaned against a fence and thought hard. *Where else would she go? Where have we been together?*

The hayride. Rebecca had had no idea that was a miserable day for him. She had loved every minute of hanging at his britches and babbling away. And they had walked home together that afternoon—

Tearing up the road past Thorndike Hill like a mad dog, Josiah made for Solomon's Hill, retracing every step they had taken that day. He climbed trees and looked down. He crawled through the underbrush and whispered her name. He even tore apart piles of browning leaves, thinking she may have hidden in one and fallen asleep.

But when he got to the top of Solomon's Hill, he hadn't seen one trace of her. His mouth had gone dry, and the sickening dread had taken total control of his stomach. *Her father was killed by Indians,* one of the nagging voices kept screaming in his head. Why had he ever used the Indians to frighten her? Why had he ever wanted to frighten her at all?

But the sick feeling only slowed him down, and he tossed his head from side to side to get rid of the voices as he tore down Solomon's Hill. Joseph Putnam was always kind to her. Maybe she'd gone to him. And she *had* been to Israel Porter's before. She would know the way—

He had just reached the other side of Davenport Hill when

he heard a voice shouting to him from a house. Josiah dove behind a low log fence that was for some reason covered with pine branches and held his breath. Nobody must see him. Whose house was that, anyway?

Josiah looked around to get his bearings, and his heart sank. He was right behind John Putnam's farm. Eleazer—or even John Putnam himself—was sure to be out in the fields.

Josiah dug himself farther under the branches, but several of them toppled off and Josiah realized that someone must have laid them there on purpose to cover the fence. He pulled a bunch of them over him and peeked out. Two pairs of footsteps approached to the tune of excited voices.

"I tell you, I saw somebody out here by the trap!" said one voice. Eleazer, Josiah was sure.

"What would he be doing up here?" said the other. Jonathon Putnam.

Do these boys never stay on their own farms and work? Josiah thought. *No wonder Papa says their crops are all in a shambles.*

Their feet stopped just short of the fence Josiah had climbed over. From between the pine needles, Josiah saw Jonathon scratching his head. "He's a sissy schoolboy. He should be with Uncle Joseph right now. I don't think you saw him, you ninny."

Josiah heard a popping sound as Jonathon whacked Eleazer on the head. *The Putnams seem to do a great deal of that,* Josiah thought.

Still, the boys didn't move away but stood there discussing whether or not Josiah Hutchinson was actually seen skulking about their wolf trap. The longer they talked, the harder it was for Josiah to keep still, especially with something poking him in the back. Stealthily, he reached his hand under him and rolled it aside. It felt like an ear of corn that had long since started to rot. What on earth—a fence covered with loose branches, with corn cobs and rotting apples tossed inside—

Josiah stifled a gasp. He was inside their wolf trap.

"I'd best get back to the wood chopping or there will be a whipping in store for me," Eleazer said. "You'd better get home with your load, too."

"Aye, but if he's out here, I'd surely like to find him," Jonathon said tightly.

Josiah groaned silently. Jonathon's footsteps weren't taking him back in the direction of his uncle's house but instead were circling the wolf pen Josiah was crouched in. Eleazer's steps joined him, and together they went around—once, twice, three times. Finally, Jonathon stopped, and it sounded as if Eleazer rammed into his back.

"Idiot!" Jonathon said, and then, "Is this the way you arranged these branches?"

"Aye."

"Just this way?"

Before Eleazer could answer, the branches were swept away—and Josiah was exposed, crouched at the bottom of the wolf pen.

"Wolf!" Jonathon Putnam cried and began to hiss through his teeth.

"What are you doing in our trap, Josiah Hutchinson?" Eleazer demanded.

"I'm not crowding out the wolves, that's sure," Josiah said, more bravely than he felt. "You won't catch any wolves in this trap, so I might as well nap here, eh?"

"We have already caught a wolf here," Eleazer said importantly. "That very net fell on him as he was swallowing the hooks and then—whack!—he was dead. Or hadn't you noticed the—"

Jonathon hit him on the head again, and Eleazer was quiet, though scowling. Jonathon then reached down and grabbed the back of Josiah's vest and pulled him up. In the process, Elizabeth tumbled to the ground. Josiah kicked himself loose and reached down to grab the doll, but Jonathon was faster.

"What have we here, Eleazer? I think I spy a poppet." He looked with mocking wide eyes at Josiah. "Still playing with dolls, *Mistress* Hutchinson? I knew you were a sissy schoolboy, but my, my—"

Josiah made another grab for the doll, but Jonathon tossed her neatly to Eleazer, who caught her in midair. When Josiah took that chance to turn and run, Jonathon made a dive for him and brought him down with both arms wrapped around his knees.

"The net, Eleazer!" he shouted. "Get the wolf net!"

The thought that they planned to trap him in their wolf pen didn't come to Josiah in words—it came in an image of him tangled in a net with his legs tied together while Rebecca got farther and farther away. Energy shot through him, and he kicked at Jonathon, then bit him and pulled a handful of his hair. But wiry Jonathon Putnam held on until Josiah was tied at his ankles and wrists, gagged, and tossed into the wolf pen with a net over him and branches strewn across it.

"What will we do with him now?" Eleazer said.

"We'll wait until we can gather the others together and then we'll all decide." Jonathon dusted his hands on the back of his britches. "But I think Uncle John will want to know that a Hutchinson boy was trying to steal one of the wolves that was to our credit by all rights, eh?"

Eleazer laughed as if that brilliant thought were his idea.

"Perhaps your Indian squaw will come and save you," Jonathon hissed, and together the cousins walked away.

"What about the doll?" Eleazer said as they went.

"I'll keep it," Jonathan said. "It may come in handy, eh?"

Josiah waited until he could no longer hear their boots before he wriggled upright and kicked off most of the branches. But then all he could do was lie there—and stare at the gray autumn sky—and pray that somebody else would find Rebecca.

He and God hadn't figured it out, after all. So much for Joseph Putnam's faith in him. So much for proving that he was anything at all—except a load of trouble for everyone.

At that thought, Josiah's eyes sprang wide open. No—he had to do something. Rocking his body from side to side, he began to thrash.

By the time the sun was straight overhead and straining to push its rays through the autumn mist, Josiah had managed to get all of the branches off him and the coarse net away from his face, just by wiggling and squirming. But the knots

on his ankles and wrists were tight, and it seemed the harder
he pulled on them, the more they cut into his skin.

He spent the rest of the afternoon chewing at the dirty rag
they'd tied around his mouth. When the sun began to disappear behind Davenport Hill, he had gnawed only a tiny hole
in the thick cloth.

Don't start crying, he told himself harshly. *You have to
think—you have to pray—you can't be a baby and cry.*

But it's your fault Rebecca ran away, screamed another
voice in his head. *If she can't be found and Aunt Esther dies
from grief, it's your fault.*

Somehow over these voices, he heard a crackling noise,
and he shook his head to clear it. Something or someone was
approaching the wolf pen.

The footsteps were too light to be a person's. Josiah
decided they must belong to a deer. The smell of food in the
pen, even though it was rotting, was sure to bring any number
of animals. Josiah was surprised the squirrels and raccoons
hadn't already visited him.

And then it was there—so close he could hear the animal
sniffing the air to get his scent. Standing over him, looking
deep into the pen, was a wolf.

For a minute, Josiah's heart seemed to stop. He couldn't
run. He couldn't scream. He could do nothing but wait for
this wild animal to eat him alive.

But the wolf didn't move. His face was soft and very young, not
wildly frightened like the one they'd seen near Fair Maid's Hill—
the one whose tail was left hanging on their door. Josiah wondered
for a sad moment if that wolf had been this baby's father.

The wolf tilted his head as he stared at Josiah and sniffed again.

It occurred to Josiah that the wolf was just curious. He was just a boy, like Josiah—and he just wanted to know who *this* animal was. *If you could just get to know one,* Josiah had thought once. *If you could just put your hand out for a wolf to lick or look into his eyes and find out what he was thinking.* Josiah tossed his head to try to get the gag off. He really wanted to say something to him.

But the pup was startled by the sudden movement, and he pulled back. Then he searched Josiah's face with his eyes. And for an instant—for a magic moment—their eyes met.

I want to know who you are, the wolf's eyes seemed to say, *but you're different from me—and I'm afraid.*

"They said they left him here!" cried a voice from the hill.

The moment passed. The wolf pup's ears pricked up and almost without a sound, he was gone.

Josiah looked toward the hill. The voice sounded like Abigail Williams's pinched, whiny tone. He stayed quiet. It wasn't until he heard Hope join in that he started to moan loudly through the cloth.

"In their wolf pit, you say?" Hope said.

"Aye! I knew you'd think it was funny, Hope!"

"Hhuupphh!" Josiah managed to get out.

There was silence at the base of the hill. "What was that?" Abigail said.

"Abby, you know I can't hear even half of what you can!"

Aye, Abigail, Josiah thought angrily, *you've made fun of her for it enough times.*

He "hhuupphh'ed" loudly again, and this time Abigail ran to him. Hope was right beside her as they leaned on the logs and looked down at him. Abigail's narrow green eyes disappeared as she doubled over the fence with laughter.

"They've caught themselves a wolf all right!" she hooted. "Only this one's just a pup!"

Hope stared down at him, and Josiah could see the anger gathering in her eyes. She didn't say a word. She didn't have to.

Abigail tried to stop laughing and grabbed Hope by the arm. "What do you think they'll do with this pup?"

"Nothing," Hope said grimly, "because he isn't going to be here when they get back."

She jumped lightly over the low fence and ripped the gag off Josiah's mouth. Abigail was immediately sober.

"What are you doing?" she said.

"I'm getting him loose," Hope said.

Abigail put her hands on her hips. "Hope Hutchinson, you said you wanted me to bring you here so you could have a good laugh, too. What are you about?"

"I'm about rescuing my brother from your wretched friends." Hope tore loose the last knot around Josiah's wrists, and he sat up and went for the leg knots. Hope stood up to face Abigail.

"So you were only pretending to be my friend—to get information from me," Abigail said, her voice pinched tightly.

"You're a smart girl, Abigail," Hope said. "That's exactly right."

"You are a wretched, scheming, lying—fraud!" Abigail screamed.

Hope smiled. "Well, you would know about that now, wouldn't you?"

Josiah stood up and grabbed Hope's hand. "Come on," he said into her ear.

"Good evening, Abigail," Hope said as they tore up and over Davenport Hill.

"You won't get away with this, Hope Hutchinson!" Abigail screamed from below. "We'll get you—just you wait and see if we don't!"

Josiah was sure they would at least try, but that didn't matter now. He had to find Rebecca.

✢ ✤ ✢

Chapter Twelve

They didn't stop running until they reached the top of Thorndike Hill, and Hope bent over to catch her breath. Her shoulders heaved, with anger as much as anything, Josiah knew.

"Has she—has Rebecca come home yet?" he asked.

Hope stood up and shook her head. "It's getting dark, Josiah. Now Mama and Papa will be worried over you, too. Please—won't you come home and then we can all search for her?"

"It's my fault she's gone!" Josiah said. "I have to bring her home."

Hope folded her arms across her chest. "And what if you can't?"

Josiah had wondered the same thing all afternoon as he'd stared at the sky, and now he chased both her thought and his out of his head. "I will find her."

Hope looked hard at him, and then she tossed her black curls. "All right, then. I'll go home and tell them you're safe. Aunt Esther is still resting—she doesn't even know Rebecca is missing—so there's that to be thankful for."

And very little else, Josiah thought.

"But if you don't find her by the time it's completely dark, promise you'll come home, eh?"

Josiah didn't answer. He couldn't make that promise.

With a sigh, Hope ran down the hill. Josiah watched her until she was swallowed up by the twilight. Then he stood at the highest point of the hill and looked down on the village. He'd been everywhere. There was no place else to look in Salem. If only Rebecca had said something to someone—left word in some way. But she never gave answers—she only asked questions.

Except once.

Josiah came to attention like one of Thomas Putnam's militia men.

Where would you run to? Josiah had asked her.

I'd run to God, she had said, *I'd run straight to God.*

Wildly, Josiah looked around, as if he would find God's house there in the valley below.

And there it was. The Meeting House. Right across from the Hutchinson farm. It was as close to God's house as he could get right now, and Josiah tore toward it. His feet barely touched the ground until he got there.

It was a Friday night. There were no meetings of the church committee tonight. No tail end of Lecture Day. No cleaning of the Meeting House for the Sabbath. The church was as dark as a cave as Josiah crept up the steps and peered through the crack between the doors.

No little girl would shut herself up in a place that black and lonely, Josiah thought. He would have turned away if he hadn't heard her voice inside—praying.

It had to be her. No one else had a voice loud enough to carry outside the door and onto the porch. Carefully, soundlessly, so he wouldn't frighten her this time, Josiah pulled open the door and slipped inside.

It was so dim, he couldn't see her at first. And so he followed the sound of her droning voice to the spot where she sat, halfway up on the west side, where she might have sat in her own church in Maine or Hingham with her mother, Josiah thought.

But he didn't go to her right away. He stood in the back of the Meeting House and listened.

"Father in heaven," she said in a voice that was hoarse and croaky, "please protect us from the Indians. My papa didn't mean to kill them—but Mama said he had to. Please don't let them kill us. Please don't let them kill Mama—or Joshua. I love Mama." She stopped and for a minute Josiah thought she was choking. But it was a sob, the big gulping kind, that had stopped her. She caught her breath and went on—and her words fell on Josiah like an ax.

"Please, please, please, Father God," she said, "please protect my Joshua. I love Joshua."

Josiah took the center aisle in three steps and was at her side on the bench before she could even look up. The face that turned to his had eyes swollen shut—only red-rimmed poke holes looked out at him. In her lap, her hands twisted around her nightdress, bunching it in a wet ball between her fingers.

"Joshua!" she cried.

She flung her chubby arms around his neck, and Josiah knew why her voice sounded so raspy and hoarse. She had been sitting in the Meeting House, praying to God all day.

"Come on, Rebecca." He peeled her arms away but held on to both of them. "We must go home. They're worried about you there."

She didn't try to pull away, but terror chased across her puffy face. "We can't go there, Joshua! The Indians—!"

In all the time he'd lain in the wolf pit, Josiah hadn't thought for a minute about what he would tell her when he found her. Now the words stuck in his throat and the voices screamed, and he could only put his arms around her chunky body and pick her up.

"Don't worry," he told her. "It wasn't the Indians. It's safe. You have to trust me, Rebecca."

Though there's no reason why you should, he thought bitterly.

But Rebecca clasped her hands around his neck and gratefully nuzzled her face into his. A day of painful praying, and all it took to get her back to the house was his word. Josiah squeezed her against him and began to make his way out of the pew.

But suddenly the Meeting House door creaked open, and the thin silhouette of a man appeared in the doorway. Josiah didn't have to see the face to know it was Reverend Parris. He dumped Rebecca to the ground and fell beside her.

"Shh!" he hissed into her ear. "We must be quiet. He can't find us."

There were no questions. Rebecca lay like a lump. Josiah wasn't even sure she was breathing.

The Reverend Samuel Parris quickly made his way up the aisle toward the front of the church, passing them without a glance. Rebecca looked at Josiah out of her bloated eyes, and Josiah put his finger to his lips. She smiled and nodded.

"It has come to my attention," Reverend Parris cried out in his shrill voice.

Josiah jumped and Rebecca clutched his vest. For one horrible moment, Josiah thought they'd been discovered. But then Reverend Parris ranted on, and Josiah recognized the tone and the words. The minister was practicing his sermon.

"It's all right," Josiah whispered.

"You may think it strange," Reverend Parris went on, "that I should preach a sermon in God's church about the failure of His people to pay the taxes necessary for my salary as your minister. But I must remind you that Jesus Himself was betrayed—by one Judas Iscariot. Why, then, should betrayal not happen to a lesser man?"

Josiah shivered. There was something very cold and empty about this sermon. Josiah always felt warm when people talked about God in the right way. But God surely seemed far away right now.

"Jesus Himself was disgraced—as I have been," Reverend Parris cried into the lonely darkness. "He was reviled—as I have been. He was humiliated—as I have been—"

He reached the height of his emotion, and his hand

slapped heavily on the lectern he was leaning on. That was too much for Rebecca. She put her hands over her pinched-tight little mouth, but the squeal of terror exploded through her lips anyway.

The minister's last words hung lifelessly in the air, and he gasped. "Who's there?" he cried. "Who is there, spying on me?"

Josiah pushed Rebecca to the end of the bench and pointed her toward the back of the church. "Run, Rebecca!" he hissed in her ear. "Run to the barn as fast as you can!"

"You, too, Joshua?" she said in a hoarse whisper.

"Aye! Now go!"

Josiah was on her heels as she scrambled from the floor and stumbled heavily toward the door. Josiah knew Reverend Parris was coming down the aisle by now, and he plowed behind Rebecca. By some miracle, she made it out the door without tripping and sprawling spread-eagle on the church floor.

But Josiah himself was not so lucky. Just as he reached the doorway, he felt the stiff hand of Reverend Parris close around his wrist.

"Who are you?" he demanded.

With a sigh that came from the toes of his boots, Josiah turned around. Reverend Parris squinted at him through the gloom, and his thin, pointy eyebrows shot up.

"It's young Hutchinson, is it not?" he said.

"Aye, sir," Josiah said weakly.

Reverend Parris let go of his arm, but his eyes kept Josiah rooted to the spot. "What are you about here?"

"I—I came to see—to see if a prayer of mine had been answered, sir." From the twisted look on the minister's face,

Josiah knew his answer had completely baffled him, but he couldn't bring himself to lie anymore. Not after all that had happened today.

To his surprise, Reverend Parris nodded, although his eyes were still suspicious as he searched Josiah's face.

"Aye," he said, "I came for much the same reason." He looked around the shadowy church. "I have prayed and prayed for this congregation, and every day I come here to see if my prayers have been answered. But to this day—20 percent of the church tax for the year is still unpaid, do you know it?"

Josiah shook his head. Reverend Parris's voice was reaching sermon level, and Josiah steeled himself for the blast.

"They have no respect for the dignity and status of a minister here. They are not concerned about my honor or my shame." His face whipped back to Josiah as if he expected him to answer.

"Aye, sir," Josiah mumbled. He had begun to feel a little frightened of this angry, tortured man. Perhaps if he agreed enough, Reverend Parris would soon just grab him by the ear and drag him home. Even that would be better than this strange scene.

"I believe that the church is a refuge against devils and their human companions. Do you believe that, young Hutchinson?"

Josiah wanted to say that he didn't. His father had always told him the church should be a brotherhood of saints, a way of changing the community, not escaping from it. But Josiah nodded. God, he was sure, wouldn't mind this lie.

"Then, why is it," Reverend Parris shouted, "that since the

summer, not a single Salem Village man or woman has sought membership in this church? I fear for these people. I truly fear for them—because of the wrath of God that will come on them."

He was strangely silent for a moment, and Josiah closed his eyes to try to unscramble the thoughts that threatened to tear his brain apart. This God Reverend Parris was talking about, this wasn't the God Josiah had come to know, the One Joseph Putnam urged him to go to whenever he'd done something terrible. Josiah knew he needed forgiveness for what he had done to Rebecca—and he was willing to take any punishment. But *wrath*? Was he supposed to be *afraid* of God?

"It's the Porters—Israel and the rest—who are responsible for this!" Reverend Parris cried.

Josiah opened his eyes. Reverend Parris had sunk down onto one of the benches, as if he planned to stay there a while. Josiah smothered a groan.

"The Porters are evil people—wretched souls who will burn—" The minister cut himself short and looked at Josiah. "Your father is not like them."

Josiah felt his mouth falling open. He'd always thought Reverend Parris hated his father.

"He refuses to pay my salary or provide my firewood, but I know he has some small measure of respect for me." The minister suddenly seemed possessed with an idea, and his eyes burned as he stood up and shook Josiah's arm. "Go you home, boy, and see you tell your father this. Tell him I was merciful to you tonight, and that I ask for no punishment for your being here. You tell him that. That should raise me somewhat in his esteem."

And with that he stood to his feet and went back up the aisle. Josiah thought for a second that Reverend Parris must be the loneliest person in Salem Village. But only for a second. Before two seconds passed, Josiah was out the door.

✠ ⬦ ✠

Chapter Thirteen

The Hutchinson farm was only a short run from the Meeting House, but Josiah didn't go straight to the barn. He crept up to the house first and peeked carefully into the kitchen window. Mama and Papa sat by the fire, facing each other and talking with serious faces. Hope stood apart from them, wringing her hands. Josiah breathed a sigh of relief as she glanced toward the window and saw him there. He pointed and mouthed "barn." Casting a wary glance at her parents, she nodded.

When Josiah got to the barn, Rebecca was perched in the loft, half covered in hay and looking down at the oxen with worried eyes. Josiah hushed the voices in his head. He had so much to explain to her. They might be grown-ups themselves before he could get it all said.

He took the wooden ladder in two steps and plopped down beside her. She put her arms around his neck. That still felt funny to him, but he let her do it.

"You're safe now, Rebecca," he said.

"Indians won't come back?" she said in her too-loud voice, now crispy around the edges from the day's praying.

"No."

"Never," said Hope. She joined them in the hayloft and ran her hand across Rebecca's nightcap.

"In fact," Josiah said, "there were never any—"

"Never any reason to be afraid because Joshua and I will always take care of you," Hope said quickly. She shot Josiah a warning look he didn't understand. "All you have to do now is crawl into bed beside your mama, and everything will be all right—for always."

Rebecca didn't answer. Her body had already sagged into sleep in Hope's lap.

"Why didn't you let me tell her?" Josiah whispered. "I have to tell her."

"Tell her what—that you lied to her, that you were teasing her all along, just like everyone else does?"

"That would be the truth," Josiah said. "I have to tell her the truth."

"Maybe someday." Hope tilted her chin up the way she did when she knew she was right. "But right now, she needs to trust you. If you tell her you lied to her, who can she trust?"

Josiah looked down at Rebecca miserably. "I *am* evil, you know it, Hope?"

"Oh, aye," she said sharply. "That's why you spent the whole day looking for her and risked your life in a wolf pen and—where did you find her, anyway?"

"In the Meeting House, praying," Josiah said. "And Reverend Parris came in to practice his sermon and almost caught her. I think he scared her worse than the Indians."

Hope giggled softly. "What was she praying about?"

A lump that felt dangerously like tears rose up in the back of his throat. He swallowed hard. "She was praying for me—so I wouldn't be hurt by the Indians."

"Ach."

Hope brushed her finger over a string of Rebecca's acorn-colored hair that fell limply across her face. "You know, Josiah, she's more loyal than any of our other friends."

"Aye." A tear splashed down on Josiah's hand, and he wiped it furiously on his britches.

"I think we need each other, we three." Hope laughed then and punched Josiah softly on the arm. "We make a merry band, eh?"

"What do you mean?" Josiah said.

"I don't think the Putnams are finished with us yet—and Abigail surely isn't. We'll be a merry band against them."

Josiah stared at her, and he couldn't help laughing himself. "You—me—and *Rebecca*?"

"Aye. We haven't much choice, Josiah," she said. "We're all we have."

Rebecca woke up when they carried her into the kitchen, and she was confused as Mama and Papa hugged her and passed her back and forth, searching for hidden bruises and broken bones. By then she was half awake and began to whimper.

"I want Elizabeth," she cried.

Josiah's heart fell to his knees.

"Who is Elizabeth?" Mama said.

But Papa held Rebecca up in front of him and said, "Now, you can't go up to your mama like that. Have we no corn for popping? That would surely wipe those tears away, eh?"

Josiah and Hope looked at each other in disbelief. Popping corn was a treat saved for only the most special occasions. They usually had to persuade Papa to let them do it, and now he was suggesting it. Hope dove for the shaker before he could change his mind.

They sat in a half circle in front of the big fireplace, and Hope shook the long shaker over the fire until the hard kernels of corn sprang open into puffs of snow. But before she had even eaten a mouthful, Rebecca was asleep again in Mama's lap with a trail of popcorn running down the front of her now very grimy nightdress, bear-cub snores puffing out of her nose. Josiah felt shaky all over. He would have at least until tomorrow to think of how to explain that Elizabeth was gone forever.

"She's one of God's mysteries, that one." Papa looked down at his niece. "Now—suppose you tell me why she ran away today, eh?"

Papa looked first at Hope and then at Josiah from under the hoods of his thick, sandy eyebrows. His eyes weren't angry, but the uneasiness that Josiah always felt when he disappointed his father curled around in his stomach anyway. He had such a hard time putting his actions and the reasons for them into words. It was what his father said next that finally got his tongue moving.

"There is a cold, silent war going on here in Salem Village," Papa said, "and it can do more damage to our lives than the Indians or the wolves or those people in Boston, because I think this war has caught up even our children. You both can be of some help to me in stopping it." His blue eyes pierced through them. "But you must be honest. You cannot be fearful of punishment. You must simply tell the truth."

The only sound in the kitchen was the steady snapping of the popcorn in the shaker. Hope studied her hands and Josiah the toes of his boots. Papa leaned back in his chair, crossed his arms over his broad chest, and waited.

Josiah tilted up his chin and looked at his father. "It's my fault she ran away."

"Let you tell me about it, then," Joseph Hutchinson said.

Josiah began to talk, and in sentences that sometimes stumbled and fell over themselves, he told him everything—how he had told Rebecca stories about the Indians and the wolves and the oxen to get her to leave him alone and then to frighten her because she had been the cause of his being miserable—how the Putnam boys added to his misery by following him and chasing him and bullying him—how it all came to a head with Rebecca's disappearance and how he had searched for her and spent most of the day in John Putnam's wolf pen, only to find her where she had once told him she'd go. He even told him that Reverend Parris had been "merciful" to him by letting him go.

Josiah didn't leave out anything, and when he was finished he tried to look right into his father's eyes. They were unhappy, but they weren't angry, and Josiah shook a little with relief.

"I know some things, too, Papa, that might help," Hope said. She swallowed hard. "But when I tell you, you'll also find out some things about me that—that won't make you happy."

"Aye," Papa said quietly. "Go on, then."

So Hope told how she was angry with Papa for not letting her work in the Proctors' inn with Sarah, and twice as angry for having to watch out for Rebecca—how she became friends with Abigail when her own friends shunned her because of Rebecca—and how, as a result, she'd found out that it was probably Thomas Putnam who paid John Indian to hang a warning sign on their door to frighten them.

As Hope pieced her story together, the fragment of another conversation fell into Josiah's mind. *We've already caught a wolf here,* Eleazer had said. *That very net fell on him as he was swallowing the hooks and then—whack!—he was dead. Or hadn't you noticed the—*

"I think I know where he got the wolf's tail," Josiah said.

Papa looked at him sharply.

"They caught a wolf at John Putnam's—at least Eleazer said so."

"The Putnams are the cause of this 'war' you're talking about, aren't they, Papa?" Hope said.

The lines along the sides of Papa's face grew deeper, and Josiah thought he looked very, very tired. "Aye," their father said wearily. "Because the Putnams are at war with themselves, and I think perhaps that's the worst kind of war there is."

Josiah nodded. Papa, as usual, was absolutely right.

Hope thought so, too, it appeared. She got up from her chair and went to stand in front of her father. Her face was white and pinched as if she were afraid, but her voice was strong as she spoke.

"Papa," she said, "I'm sorry I was so angry with you—it made me do stupid things. I'll take whatever punishment you give me without a word, I promise."

To everyone's amazement, Papa took both of Hope's hands in his and spoke in a quiet voice. "We have a stern society here in Massachusetts. We Puritans are known for our rules. But we follow those rules to please God because we have faith that He knows what's best for us, eh?"

"Aye," Hope said uncertainly.

"I try to follow God's example in being your earthly father, Hope," he said. "I make rules for your own good, and I expect you to follow them because you have faith that I know what's best for you." He looked down at his big, rough hands for a moment. "I myself have made many mistakes when I was angry. Just today, I marched in on Thomas Putnam down at Ingersoll's Ordinary and demanded to know if he put the wolf's tail on our door." He chuckled softly. "I now owe Nathaniell Ingersoll for breaking one of his tables. And what good did it do me? Thomas denied that he did it—and now I find out that quite truthfully he himself didn't, though he had a hand in it." Papa shook his head. "I cannot judge you, Hope. I can only pray that you've learned from this."

Hope brushed a tear from her cheek and nodded. "Aye, sir."

"Aye, sir," Josiah mumbled, too.

When Josiah climbed into his cot, he realized how much his body ached to lie down. His eyelids were very nearly closed for good when Hope hissed to him from the window. Rebecca was tucked soundly into Hope's bed so that she wouldn't disturb Aunt Esther, and Hope was perched on the trunk with her legs pulled up under her nightdress.

"Can we talk about it tomorrow?" Josiah said.

"Nay, there isn't time," she whispered. "There's a war on, and we've things to do."

"We do?" His brain stretched awake, and he hurried to the window to join her.

"Papa said we could help, and I think we should."

"By doing what?"

"I'm not sure yet, but it's certain we can't do it alone."

Josiah tucked his own legs under his nightshirt. The night air was chilly, and the conversation was making him shiver, too. "Who's to help us?" he asked.

"We haven't many choices. Sarah, Rachel, William, Ezekiel —"

"Why them? They're—they're hateful people!"

"Who else, then?"

Stubbornly, Josiah set his chin on his knees. "I don't know."

Hope thought a minute, and then her eyes began to shine. "What say you to this, Josiah? We shall plan a meeting—a time and a place to decide what's to be done. We tell them that if they want to be part of the—" She stopped to choose her next word carefully. "To be part of the adventure of helping our parents stop the village war, they must be there." She wiggled her eyebrows. "Can you imagine Ezekiel Porter turning that down? No! He'll jump at the chance to be a great warrior—and whenever he jumps, William jumps with him."

"And Sarah and Rachel?" Josiah said.

"Sarah is simple, like William. She only put me off because Rachel did, and she'll be easily won back. That will leave Rachel all by herself—and she won't be able to stand it."

Josiah looked at his big sister with admiration. He had to admit, when it came to matters of the world, she was as smart as anyone he knew.

She leaned over now and squeezed his arm. "We shall be a merry band, Josiah," she said. "Now, let you do this tomorrow—"

They had spent much of the rest of the night planning, and Josiah's eyes were heavy in the schoolroom the next day. At least he hadn't had to walk. His father had brought him in the wagon, and then stayed to explain to Joseph Putnam why he hadn't been in school the day before. Joseph didn't ask Josiah to recite many times that morning.

At dinnertime the boys usually tore home for a meal and chores before racing back to school for the afternoon. Since the hayride, Ezekiel always pulled William out of the schoolroom before Josiah could follow. But today he hung back, swinging his foot over Israel Porter's browning grass and pretending not to be waiting for Josiah. Josiah watched him from the doorway of the house and then strolled out into the yard.

"Where were you yesterday?" Ezekiel asked as Josiah passed him.

Josiah stopped and looked over his shoulder, then looked cautiously around the area. Ezekiel crouched in and William with him.

"I can't tell you right now," Josiah said in a low voice.

"Why not?" Ezekiel said in a voice just as low.

Josiah pretended to be annoyed. "Well, spies, of course! I'm surprised you didn't think of that, Ezekiel."

Ezekiel looked disappointed with himself and moved closer to Josiah. "Well, when can you tell us?"

Josiah slyly folded his arms. "I didn't think you would be so interested."

The big Porter eyes slammed toward the ground, and the skin seemed to pinch over Ezekiel's sharp cheekbones. "I am," he mumbled. "It's just—your cousin Rebecca is—she's crazy—and I don't want to—"

Josiah felt his face burning, and before he knew it he had Ezekiel firmly by the arm. Ezekiel's face came up sharply and he froze in Josiah's grasp.

"Now see here, Ezekiel Porter," Josiah said. "My cousin is not crazy. She may be slow but she's a lot smarter than you are in some ways. She would never push her friend off on the Putnams, just because she was afraid."

"Afraid!" Ezekiel said fiercely.

"Aye—afraid. I learned some time ago that people hate what they don't understand. It's very simple, Ezekiel. Rebecca's different, so you got scared and you hid."

Ezekiel angrily pulled his arm away, but William stepped forward and said in his soft voice, "So when will you tell us what happened yesterday?"

Again, Josiah looked around cautiously, and then he pulled two pieces of birch bark from his whistle pouch. He had scratched a message on each one with a quill pen. He handed one to William. He kept the other in his hand and looked at Ezekiel.

"Do you want one?" he said. Ezekiel shrugged and stuck out a paw. Josiah gave it to him and turned away. "If you decide to come, I shall see you there."

When he snuck a glance back at them from the bottom of the hill, they were both reading the message with hungry eyes.

By the time they reached their homes for dinner, Josiah thought, they would know that a meeting was to be held that night after supper in the loft of the Hutchinsons' barn. Anyone who wanted to be part of the adventure of helping their parents in the village war would be there.

✛ ⬦ ✛

very night as autumn went on, it grew dark earlier. The sun had already left most of the village in golden silhouette as Hope, Rebecca, and Josiah sat in the hayloft waiting. The farm was quiet except for the soft grunts of the cattle—sounds that made Rebecca edge closer to Josiah.

"Did you give them hay, Joshua?" she said loudly as she eyed the oxen from behind his shoulder.

"Once you tell her something, there is no erasin' it," Hope said.

Josiah just nodded. He'd already told Rebecca that the bandits had taken Elizabeth but that he would get her back. His promise was the only thing that kept her from crying for the lost doll. She told Josiah bravely, with tear-filled eyes, that he shouldn't worry—she would be fine until he got her back.

Right now he was more worried about something else. It

was getting darker and colder and still no Sarah and William, no Rachel and Ezekiel.

"Do you think they even showed the messages to their sisters?" Hope sighed. "I knew I should have gotten the notes to the girls, and then they'd be sure to come. You can always depend on girls more than you can boys—"

Before Josiah could object to that, his ears picked up a sound, and he waved for Hope to be quiet. He heard it again, outside the barn. Quickly, he stuck his hand into his pouch and dug for his whistle. He blew three long toots and listened.

He was answered by three short toots. William.

Josiah blew three more times, and then the barn door creaked open. In a few seconds, William and Sarah were in the loft with them.

Hope's face broke into a smile. "I knew you'd come," she whispered to Sarah.

Sarah smiled back and squeezed her arm, and Josiah thought Hope looked happier than he'd seen her in a long time.

But he also saw Sarah glance uneasily at Rebecca and then look away. William didn't look at anyone but sat silently next to his sister and studied his knees.

"Are Rachel and Ezekiel coming?" Hope asked.

Sarah shrugged. "I don't know. I didn't ask them."

Hope looked surprised. "You came on your own, then?"

Sarah's pale face flushed pink, and she, too, took a sudden interest in her knees. "Aye. I missed you. I was just waiting for an invitation."

"Shh!" Josiah said suddenly. He'd heard another whistle.

So had William. Both of them crouched and listened. Out of the now gray-black night came two long toots and one short. Josiah answered with three long—while Hope rolled her eyes at Sarah. In a moment, Ezekiel scrambled up to the loft, with Rachel behind him.

Ezekiel plopped casually down next to William and looked at everyone with wide, innocent eyes. Rachel looked at no one, and she sniffed as she sat on the edge of the loft and swung her legs.

"So what's this all about?" Ezekiel surveyed them all over his sharp cheekbones. "Some kind of big plan or something?"

Hope looked at Josiah, who nodded. When it came to laying things on the line, Hope was the person for the job. She cleared her throat and narrowed her snapping black eyes at Ezekiel.

"Now, let's get one thing straight," Hope said. "We have decided that we should help our parents in the cold, silent war going on in this village in whatever way we can. We have formed a merry band, and we are here tonight to make a plan of action. We have invited the four of you to join us."

"And who is 'us'?" Rachel said. It was the first thing she'd said since she arrived, and everyone jumped at the stiffness in her voice.

"'Us' means Josiah and me," Hope said. "And Rebecca."

A chill settled over the hayloft that set the hair on the back of Josiah's neck standing straight up.

"You see," Hope went on, "we want only loyal people in our merry band. People who don't turn hateful when they're afraid of something they don't understand. People who would never turn their backs on their friends. That describes the members so far."

There was another silence. Josiah watched them all. Sarah looked like she was ready to cry, and William like he was about to be sick. They were ashamed for sure, Josiah thought. The merry band could count on them, even though they were as frightened as rabbits. Ezekiel looked at Hope like he didn't know what she was talking about, although Josiah saw him cut his eyes toward Rebecca, the way you did at a snake to be sure it was heading the other way.

Only Rachel looked as if she had a decision to make. Hope waited, smoothing her skirts and tucking her rebellious curls under her cap.

Finally, Rachel sat up straight. "All right, then. If that's the way you shall have it, so be it."

Hope nodded as if that would be good enough for now. Josiah dove under a pile of hay and brought out several large pieces of birch bark and two quill pens. Paper was scarce in Salem Village, but bark would do just fine for what they had to do.

"So—you say there's a war going on?" Sarah said nervously.

"A silent war, my papa says," Hope told her. "People—well, the Putnams—are doing sneaky things just to frighten others—perhaps to get them to move away, or maybe just to scare them into doing things their way." Quickly, she told the story of the Indian sign on the door and all that had happened to Josiah and Rebecca as a result, and when she was finished, even Rachel's mouth was gaping.

"But what can we do about it?" Rachel said. "Do we hang wolves' tails on the Putnams' doors?"

"No!" Josiah cried.

"If we do something like that, we're just as sinful as they are," Hope said. "It has to be something that shows them we aren't afraid of them—"

"We are!" Sarah said.

Ezekiel snorted.

"You're not?" Hope said to him.

"Of course not!"

"Good, then. We'll remember that." Her eyes twinkled at Josiah as she continued. "We have to do something that doesn't hurt anyone, but that shows them what our side stands for."

"You have an idea?" Rachel said.

Hope pressed her lips together grimly. "No."

Slowly, Josiah raised his hand, the way the boys always did in Joseph Putnam's class.

"Josiah?" Hope said.

"Well, what about the wolves?"

"What about them?" Ezekiel said. "You are crazy with the wolves, Josiah!"

"Hush now! Hear him out," said Hope.

"What I mean is," Josiah said, forming his words slowly and carefully, "they used a wolf to try and frighten us—well, to try and frighten my father into joining the militia. Papa doesn't believe the Indians are a threat, and Thomas Putnam was trying to make him believe they are. What they do to the wolves is cruel. So, by saving the wolves—"

His voice trailed off, and they all looked at him blankly. But Hope began to nod. "Go on."

"What if we were to take apart all of the Putnams' wolf

traps—the ones with the hooks especially. All of them have them except Edward. It wouldn't be hard to do—I spent a whole day in one so I know how they're put together."

"But how could we do that without being caught?" Sarah's eyes were already rimmed in red at the thought of being placed in the stocks.

But Ezekiel leaned forward, and his wide Porter eyes were gleaming. "We would have to do it in the dark of a moonless night. But it could be done."

"I know just the night, too." Rachel's eyes, too, were suddenly shining. "Cousin Constance and Joseph are to be married in just three days in Salem Town. None of us will be going—but all of the adults will. Most of the village will be ours."

A slow smile spread over Hope's face, and because she was smiling, Sarah began to smile, too, though shakily. Ezekiel was already rubbing his hands together, and even the quiet wheels in William's mind seemed to be turning. Only Josiah frowned.

"But we have to remember the rules," he said.

"Oh, the little boy becomes the royal governor!" Rachel said, wagging her head.

"Hush now and let him speak," Hope said. Everyone fell silent. "What are the rules, Josiah?"

Josiah took a huge breath. He hated it when he had all those eyes staring at him.

"No lying to our parents," he said. "And no hurting anyone and no doing anything—God wouldn't want us to do."

It was quiet again, but one by one the heads began to nod.

"All right, then, merry band." Hope's cheeks were crimson

with excitement. "We have plans to make."

The pieces of birch bark were laid out in a clear space on the floor, and the merry band all flopped on their stomachs while Josiah lit a lantern and hung it from a rafter. Only Rebecca hung back, and when Josiah joined the group, she tugged at his britches.

"Joshua," she whispered loudly.

Josiah pulled her aside, away from the others. "What is it?"

"We're going to help the wolves?" she said.

"Aye."

"Me, too?"

Josiah glanced over at the merry band who were already in the midst of their great plans. He blew out some air. There was something she could do—he'd see to that. He at least owed her that much.

"You, too," he said.

Her face puckered. "But what if I don't know how?"

"Of course you'll know how," Josiah said. "And I'll be right there with you."

Her face broke into a puzzle of creases as she smiled.

It only took one evening to discover that three days was a very short time to prepare for battle. Hope made the assignments quickly and efficiently, and everyone swore to carry out their jobs without fail.

"Me, too!" Rebecca chimed in.

Everyone looked at her doubtfully. Ezekiel even gave an almost-silent groan. But Josiah said, "Aye. You, too."

The very next day, the work began.

While Joseph Putnam drilled William and Ezekiel on their times tables, Josiah drew endless diagrams of the wolf pit he'd spent a day in. And while Josiah was reading for Joseph, William and Ezekiel studied the drawings until their eyes were crossed.

None of the boys went home for dinner for the next three days but instead volunteered to do the nut-gathering for their mothers during their free time. Most of the nuts were taken home—after the three boys' pouches were stuffed. And the tops of nut trees were perfect places for observing the locations of certain wolf traps.

All the girls offered to feed the leftovers from supper to the pigs. Unfortunately, some of the village pigs would be somewhat slender this season as the leftovers were tucked away in hiding places in barns and garden sheds.

In the evenings, Ezekiel and William sat by their family fires as always and whittled at whistles while their fathers read the Bible aloud and their mothers knitted. Sarah and Rachel watched the making of those whistles carefully, as they sewed whistle pouches for themselves. Soon they'd carry the very whistles they'd rolled their eyes over before as silly boy things—and they would have signals of their own to use.

Josiah spent his evenings in the orchard with Rebecca. Between supper and the setting of the sun, there was just enough time to show her a few of the basics of tree-climbing. Rebecca spent more time on the ground, blinking up in surprise, than she did on the branches. But Josiah could not have asked for a more enthusiastic pupil. She promised she would practice every day while he was at school, and Josiah made Hope promise to stack a pile of hay under the practice tree, just in case she really did.

The merry band met once more before battle night arrived. Their only task was to divide into teams and review the plan of action one more time.

"William and Ezekiel and Josiah should work together," Hope said. "You all know what to do, eh?"

Ezekiel nodded confidently and nudged William.

"And Sarah and you and I can work together," Rachel said. "It's perfect."

"Unless something goes wrong," Hope said. "Jonathon and Eleazer and Richard—those Putnam boys won't be going to the wedding, either. What if one of them hears us? I think I should keep watch and create a distraction if anyone comes. You and Sarah can manage without me."

"You surely are the best talker," Ezekiel said. "In case you have to talk us out of something."

"I don't know—" Sarah said, her voice beginning to tremble.

"We'll be fine, Sarah—don't be a ninny," Rachel said.

Josiah felt a tugging at his shirt sleeve, and he looked down to see Rebecca's pale blue eyes blinking up at him. "What's my job, Joshua?" she asked.

"Does she have to talk so loud?" Ezekiel whispered to Hope.

Rachel leaned forward toward Rebecca. "If you go, you'll have to learn to speak softly, or you'll give us all away."

Rebecca clapped a chubby hand over her mouth.

"Who's to be her partner, anyway?" Rachel said to Hope. "We can't send her out there alone to do—whatever."

"Would you stop talking about her like she isn't here?" Josiah snapped.

Rachel's eyes widened for a minute before she said saucily, "My, my, my—"

"All right—we must think this out," Hope said.

Josiah tilted his chin up. "You don't need to. Rebecca can be with me."

"And do what?" Ezekiel demanded.

"We need another lookout, somebody up in a tree. I'll be that, and I'll take Rebecca with me."

"It's your funeral," Ezekiel mumbled.

"Are you sure, Josiah?" Hope said.

Actually Josiah wasn't sure—he didn't even know where the idea had come from. Until now he hadn't known exactly why he was teaching Rebecca to climb trees. But he looked down at her hopeful, chubby face and said, "Of course, I'm sure. There's a place for all of us."

Hope looked at all of them solemnly. "Well, merry band, the next time we meet will be at the last edge of dark—"

"On the east side of Nathaniel Putnam's, by the marsh," Ezekiel finished for her.

Everyone nodded, but it didn't seem to be enough. Beside him, Rebecca slipped her chunky hand into Josiah's. That was the only thing that kept him from shouting out, "Perhaps we should change our minds! What if we're caught?"

Slowly, he slipped his hand into Hope's on his other side. She looked at him quickly, and then she smiled and put her hand in Ezekiel's. He looked around, bewildered, for a moment, and then slowly, as if he were sticking his hand into a pit of vipers, he curled his fingers around Rachel's. They were soon all crouched in a circle, hands entwined. Then they squeezed—and hoped the plan of action would proceed as planned.

✛ ⚜ ✛

Chapter Fifteen

The day of Joseph Putnam's wedding—and the day of the "plan"—dawned misty and gray with a hint of winter in the air.

"The frost is on the pumpkin," Josiah's father remarked as they walked toward the barn that morning. There was no school that day with Joseph Putnam preparing for the ceremony in Salem Town. And Papa was giving Josiah instructions for things to do in his absence.

"We shall be home late tonight," Papa said. "You and Hope will have to see to supper and to the wood supply—"

"Aye, sir," Josiah kept mumbling, but his mind was reeling. At least everything was going according to plan.

That was until breakfast when Aunt Esther patted her mouth with her napkin and announced, "I don't think I shall go to the wedding with you, Joseph."

Hope choked on a piece of cornbread, and Josiah tried not

to let his spoon clatter to his trencher.

"Why in heaven's name not?" Papa's sandy eyebrows went into a tangle as he frowned at her.

"I don't know Joseph Putnam well—"

"Nonsense! You knew him as a baby!"

"But this is a party, Joseph—" Aunt Esther's voice grew confused as she thrashed about for words. "I don't feel—I will be such poor company—"

"Ach!" Papa threw his hands in the air—his usual reaction when he thought someone was being silly and ridiculous.

"Esther," Mama said in her quiet voice, "no one expects you to be as carefree as the bride. But it will do you good to get out and be with people. Sometimes we have to set our troubles aside for a bit."

It was the most Mama ever said at one time, and even Rebecca seemed to know that that deserved attention. But still Aunt Esther shook her head. Josiah risked a glance at Hope. She was staring at her aunt, white-faced.

"There may be some other reason for you to go as well," Papa said. "Phillip English should be back from Boston by now. If so, he'll be there—and he may very well have some good word on the business of settling Daniel's estate."

Josiah closed his eyes.

"Perhaps I should go, then," Aunt Esther said slowly.

"And don't worry at all about Rebecca," Hope said. "We'll look after her."

"They're going to let me climb a tree!" Rebecca said.

Both Josiah's and Hope's chairs scraped back at once.

"We need more wood for the fire—" cried Josiah.

"I'll fetch more milk—" cried Hope.

And both shouted at the same time, "Rebecca, come help me!"

"They make her feel so needed," Aunt Esther said gratefully as they hauled Rebecca away.

"Aye, they're good children," Mama said.

Josiah didn't breathe normally until the wagon rocked away from the Hutchinson farm after dinner with Papa driving the oxen and Mama and Aunt Esther tucked into the back, their heads and shoulders covered against the mist. He even dashed to the edge of the property and climbed a tree to make sure they didn't change their minds at the Ipswich Road and turn back.

Then there was nothing to do but wait for darkness. They swept and gathered wood and fed the animals and made a supper no one ate except Rebecca. They would have liked having the house all to themselves had they not been counting the minutes until sunset.

Finally, the hills turned black against the sinking sun, and Hope took Rebecca upstairs to bundle her up in a dark cloak and scarf. Josiah waited impatiently in the front hall and checked his pouch 12 times for his whistle and his supply of nuts. Then, at last, they were off for Nathaniel Putnam's.

There was certainly nothing friendly about Salem Village tonight. Most of the scattered houses were dark, and the few lights that did flicker in windows had to fizzle their way through the mist that had lingered through the day and now thickened the evening. Josiah wasn't sure whether it was the gloomy night air or the uneasiness in his stomach that made him shiver. So he was glad when Rebecca crept her warm hand into his and held on. When he looked down at her, he saw her chubby face aglow with excitement.

At the edge of the marsh they stopped, and Josiah blew three long toots on his whistle. Immediately three short ones answered, and then two long and a short, and then two other sets of signals. Josiah nodded to Hope, and they moved slowly forward. Four shadowy figures rose from the tall grass.

"This will be easy as pie!" Ezekiel whispered.

"Sssssh!" Rachel hissed.

"There's no one home," Ezekiel said. "We went by the house on our way. There's not a lantern or a candle—not even a fire."

Josiah knew Hope hadn't heard any of that, so he took charge, saying to the merry band, "Let's go, then."

The mist seemed to swallow each of them up as Josiah watched them go to their places. He shivered once more and then took Rebecca by the arm. "It's time to climb that tree," he whispered.

He picked a big maple that was uphill of Nathaniel Putnam's wolf trap and managed to get Rebecca to the first place where the thick trunk forked.

"Stay here," he whispered hoarsely. She nodded, and Josiah knew an entire pack of Putnams couldn't drag her away.

He climbed several feet higher and found a sturdy branch on the back of the tree where he could stay hidden. If anyone looked up carefully he would surely be seen, for the leaves were all but gone. But Josiah knew he would see anyone long before they spotted him, and he could shinny down before they ever got to him. He settled down to see how the rest of the merry band was doing.

Through the mist he saw the shadowy forms of Sarah and Rachel standing just apart from the trap with lumpy cloth bags dangling from their waists. Josiah scanned the area. Hopefully, they wouldn't need what was inside.

He craned forward and could just see Ezekiel and William in the trap, going about their work. If all went as planned, they would first take down the chain that held the hook dipped in tallow and hand them to the girls to put in the bags with the other things. Then they would dismantle whatever other contraptions the Putnams had installed while Sarah and Rachel scattered the concealing branches. Once they were finished, William would blow a special signal on his whistle—three short blasts—and they would all know the job was done.

If anything went wrong, Hope was stationed between the trap and the house, ready to do some fast talking. And Josiah was here in the tree, ready to blow his danger signal—two long blasts—if he saw any trouble at all.

Just then a toot whistled thinly through the mist. Then two more. Nathaniel Putnam's cruel wolf trap was a thing of the past.

No one said anything until they all met at the north marsh and danced up and down, hugging each other and squealing in the backs of their throats.

"Did we free the wolves, Joshua?" Rebecca whispered

loudly. She immediately pressed both chunky hands over her mouth and looked fearfully at Rachel, but even Rachel laughed.

"I told you it was as easy as pie!" Ezekiel whispered.

"We aren't finished yet," Hope reminded them, but her eyes were already shimmering with success. "On to John Putnam's, merry band."

They squeezed hands and then split up. Josiah grabbed Ezekiel's arm and put his mouth close to his ear.

"Last time you knew there was no one around," he said softly. "This time, let me climb the tree and give you my signal before you go in, eh?"

"Aye," Ezekiel said impatiently, "but who would be out on a night like this?"

Josiah's stomach grew uneasy again as he pulled Rebecca toward the base of Davenport Hill.

He'd seen the perfect tree as he'd lain in the wolf trap that day, and he found it again quickly now and looked for a spot for Rebecca. There was really only one branch thick enough and positioned safely so they wouldn't be seen. Josiah sighed and looked at his cousin.

"We're going up there," he said, pointing. "Do just as I say."

Rebecca nodded seriously. *As if you would do anything else,* Josiah thought.

It seemed to take forever to get Rebecca's short, stocky body up the trunk and out onto the thick branch. As she plodded, Josiah imagined Ezekiel fuming in the bushes, waiting for his signal.

Rebecca finally reached the branch, straddled it, and stopped.

"Move down!" Josiah hissed. As she slowly inched her way, Josiah peered down into the darkness below. He saw the wolf trap at once, and at the same time—two other things.

Out of the bushes crept Ezekiel, followed by William. They hadn't waited for the signal, and they had nearly reached the shelter of scattered branches that concealed the trap.

But Josiah also saw that there was already a wolf in the trap.

He hadn't swallowed the hooks yet. Josiah saw them still dangling in the air above the wolf's head. But he was sniffing urgently at them, and his front paws came up off the ground as he struggled to get a closer whiff. Josiah froze. It was a small wolf with big paws and, he knew, a soft young face. It was surely his friend.

Josiah came unfrozen and yanked open his pouch. Ezekiel and William were three steps from the trap as Josiah let go with one long blast and then another.

William stopped and planted himself to the ground. Ezekiel paused only for a second, looked around, and then crept on as if he were satisfied that only he knew danger when he saw it. Again, Josiah blew—two long, furious blasts. This time Ezekiel stopped and looked at William, shrugging with annoyance.

And then Ezekiel heard it, too—the wolf dancing and pawing at the hooks just two feet away.

Fortunately the young, inexperienced wolf was enchanted by the smell of the tallow and didn't seem to notice the two-legged animals nearby. Josiah held his breath and hoped Ezekiel and William remembered the plan—what to do if a wolf was already in the trap.

From where Josiah stretched to see, it didn't appear that the wolf had yet caught his foot in the trap. If they could lure him out before he did—

Josiah watched as Ezekiel crouched farther from the trap now and blew his own whistle. Sarah and Rebecca emerged from the bedraggled cornfield, already opening their bags. Josiah had to admit that Rachel looked very sure of herself as she approached the pen.

The wolf heard her now. He came down on all fours with his ears pointed up at attention like one of Thomas Putnam's militiamen. He stood there, still as a statue, for only an instant—long enough for Rachel to dump her bag of Porter leftovers outside the pen. Sarah was slower, and Josiah could tell by the way she seemed to will her legs to move that she was terrified. But she dumped the contents of her bag farther away from the trap and then dove back into the cornfield. Rachel watched for a minute and then followed her.

The wolf sniffed the air cautiously and took a tiny mincing step toward the trail of food. Then he stopped and held his black nose up to the scent again. But instead of moving forward, he backed up, farther into the pen. His foot was inches from the trap that could enclose him in there forever.

Outside the pen, Ezekiel and William were having a feverish conversation. Ezekiel appeared to be searching for something on the ground, and then he picked up a stick. He inched on his belly toward the food and, reaching out with the stick, pushed the pile of food scraps closer to the trap. The wolf sniffed, but he backed up farther still, barely missing the trap.

Josiah put his hand in his mouth and bit down to keep from crying out. The wolf must feel a lot like he did at that moment because he began to pace inside the pen as if the pain of indecision were more than he could bear. One thing was obvious, though. He wasn't going to come outside to get that food.

He's so frightened, Josiah thought. *He's more scared of us than we are of him. And he's all alone. He needs some other wolves—maybe his mother and father—*

The idea slammed into Josiah's head like a bird hitting the side of a barn.

"Rebecca!" he hissed.

Rebecca was perched on the branch as close to him as she could get, and she looked right up into his face.

"Howl like a wolf!" he said.

"Rachel said I'm to be quiet!"

"Forget Rachel! This is Joshua telling you. Howl like a wolf—you can help!"

That was enough for Rebecca. She tilted back her head, pursed her round lips, and howled into the night.

The wolf looked up, and his frightened eyes came into focus.

"Again!" Josiah whispered.

Again, once, twice, three more times, Rebecca howled from up in the tree. On the third howl, the wolf leapt out of the pen, leaving behind the trail of food, the trap, and the cruel, swinging hooks. Josiah turned to watch his friend go, but he had disappeared into the woods—only the leaves rustled behind him.

✠ ⋅✠⋅ ✠

even bodies collapsed at the base of Hawthorne's Hill, and no one was quite sure whether they were laughing or crying, relieved or still terrified. Thomas Putnam's farm was just on the other side of the hill, but they lay in a heap on this side until their hearts could stop pounding and their breathing could slow down enough for them to speak.

Rachel was the first to talk. "God was surely with us!" she cried, her voice still shivery with nervous laughter. "He brought another wolf just in time!"

Ezekiel pulled himself to a sitting position and considered it importantly. "It must have been on top of Davenport Hill. That wolf looked right up there." He nodded like an expert. "Probably his mate."

"That wolf was too young to have a mate!" Rachel said

"It wasn't another wolf," Josiah said. "It was Rebecca."

Five pairs of disbelieving eyes slanted at him.

"I told her to howl like a wolf—and it worked. It drew the wolf right out of the pen."

"*Rebecca?*" Rachel said. Her voice wound up suspiciously. "Rebecca did that?"

"Howl like a wolf, Rebecca," Josiah said.

She did.

The five pairs of disbelieving eyes popped open.

"It's her gift," Josiah said proudly. "She can imitate any animal."

He looked down at Rebecca whose slack little mouth dropped into a smile.

"We'll hear all about it later," Hope said. "We've one more house to go, and that last one took a long time. We must be home and in our beds when our parents return from Salem Town."

"Aye!" Sarah was the first to collect herself. Nervously, she grabbed Rachel's hand. "Let's go. But if there's a wolf in this trap, I'm going to run for our inn and not stop until I get there!"

"Easy as pie," Ezekiel said, and boldly marched up the hill. He'd made a quick recovery from the scare at John Putnam's.

"Ezekiel!" Josiah whispered.

"What?"

"Wait for my signal this time, eh?"

Ezekiel gave a sulky nod and went on.

Josiah took Rebecca's hand and together they skirted Hawthorne's Hill, coming out on the west side of Thomas Putnam's farm. As soon as he saw the west field, he remembered something. One day last spring, he'd seen one of the Porters, Ezekiel's cousin Giles, taking apart one of Thomas Putnam's fences near this very spot. From the top of a tree, Josiah had watched Giles neatly put the fence back together without its pegs, so that the cattle could easily knock it down and wander off. It had always bothered him that a Porter had done such a thing, when old Israel Porter always told Papa they shouldn't lower themselves to do the kinds of things the Putnams did.

Josiah stopped at the base of the tree he'd chosen for himself and Rebecca, and a guilty pang went through him. Was what they were doing right now the same thing? Josiah ticked the rules off on his fingers. They hadn't lied to anyone. They weren't going to hurt anyone. And they weren't doing any damage. They were only undoing the damage the Putnams were trying to do—and showing them what they stood for.

"Do you want me to climb up, Joshua?" Rebecca whispered.

Josiah shook off the argument he was having with himself. "Aye. I'm right behind you."

When they reached a high, protected branch, Josiah looked down at the trap below. None of the other children were in sight around the trap, although he could see Hope clinging to one of the now-bare birch trees that lined the path from the field to Thomas Putnam's house. There were no lights in the windows and no wolves near the trap. He took out his whistle and gave the all-clear signal. Four answers came back to him.

As softly and quickly as a pair of raccoons, William and

Ezekiel emerged from the brush and scurried toward the trap. They lowered the chain, detached the hooks and set them aside for the girls to put in their bags. Then they squatted down in the shadows, and Josiah knew they were taking apart the other part of the trap. While they worked, Josiah's eyes scanned the field, the pasture, the path. He let out a gasp.

Two boyish figures were moving quickly down the path from Thomas Putnam's house, right toward Hope. The tall, lanky one with the big head Josiah knew was Jonathon Putnam, and he and his shorter companion—it could be Richard or Eleazer or Silas—walked like they had a reason to go where they were going. Jonathon took long strides, and his arms swung like two hatchets at his side, angrily cutting the air.

Josiah put his whistle to his lips with shaking fingers and gave two long, loud blasts. This time, Ezekiel didn't even stop to think. He and William skittered from the trap and disappeared into the brush.

But one look down at his sister, and Josiah's heart sank to his toes. Hope hadn't heard him. They'd never thought about Hope's half-deafness when they'd given the girls whistles and taught them the signals. Josiah tried again, blowing into his wooden whistle until he thought his lungs would burst. Hope waited, unaware, by the birch tree. In four or five good strides, Jonathon and his cousin would turn the bend in the path and meet her head-on.

Josiah thrust the whistle back in the pouch, and his fingers touched the nuts he'd packed in there to throw at the wolves to drive them away. Perhaps he could get Hope's attention with a few of them.

Josiah stood up on the branch and clung with one hand to the trunk of the tree. Rebecca gave a frightened cry.

"Shh!" Josiah said.

She clamped her hands over her mouth, but her eyes were huge with fear.

Josiah took several of the nuts in his free hand and began to hurl them. The first one zinged neatly over Hope's head. Jonathon was two steps away. Almost crying, Josiah pelted the rest of the nuts, one after another. One finally grazed Hope on the side of the cheek. She slapped her hand to her face and looked up. Through the dark mist, Josiah waved and pointed frantically.

But just then Jonathon rounded the curve—and there was Hope. Josiah watched in horror as she stepped right into the path in front of them.

Josiah sank down onto the branch beside Rebecca, his heart slamming against the inside of his chest.

"Bandits!" Rebecca whispered.

Josiah nodded.

Rebecca slapped her stubby hands over her eyes and dug her face into Josiah's shoulder, peeking through her fingers at the scene below.

Josiah couldn't hear anything that was being said, but it was apparent that William and Ezekiel and Sarah and Rachel could, because they all crawled silently out of hiding and slithered to the trap. As Hope talked on to Jonathon and—Josiah was now sure it was Thomas Putnam's son Richard—the four from the merry band worked feverishly to finish taking the trap apart.

But what was Hope saying to them? And how would she get them to go back the other way—and leave her alone?

It looked for one heavenly moment as if whatever she was saying was working. Jonathon took a few steps backward and Richard did the same. Hope pointed toward Hathorne's Hill and moved as if to go in that direction.

And then trouble hit like a bolt of lightning, and everything happened at once.

Jonathon reached inside his jacket and pulled something out. Josiah couldn't see what it was at first, but Rebecca did, and she lunged out on the branch and screamed. Jonathon was waving her doll Elizabeth in the air.

When the scream hit the night, all three faces below whipped in the direction of the tree. Hope snatched up her skirts and tried to run, but Richard grabbed her and spun her around, pinning both arms behind her back. Josiah wrapped both of his hands around Rebecca's mouth and whispered hotly, "Hush, Rebecca! The bandits will hear you!" She whimpered into his shirt as Josiah looked down in panic. Jonathon was marching down the path, and in ten seconds he would discover the rest of the merry band ripping apart his uncle's wolf trap. His eyes flew to the trap. Rachel and Sarah were gone, and William was just diving into the underbrush. Only Ezekiel was left, scattering the rest of the branches. Josiah freed one of his hands and pulled out his whistle. Sucking air from wherever it would come from, he blew two hard blasts. Ezekiel started to run, and even from the tree Josiah could hear Jonathon shouting at him. Ezekiel swerved to take him away from the place where the rest were hiding, and from behind him, Jonathon Putnam was ambushed with their barrage of flying nuts. There is nothing more surprising than getting hit squarely in the back of the head with a sailing walnut, and Jonathon was indeed surprised.

But that didn't keep him from doing an about-face and tearing toward the merry band's hiding place and right into the path of the nuts. Even though Ezekiel came up behind him and began his own firing of nuts, Jonathon plunged on. Back on the path Richard held on to Hope, even as she scratched and bit and clawed like a trapped squirrel.

"Stay here, Rebecca," Josiah said. "I've got to go down."

What he would do when he got there he had no idea. He never had to find out.

For from somewhere in that gloomy autumn night came a cry like none Josiah had ever heard. It seemed to come from the pit of someone's anger and rip through the air like a death cry.

Rebecca's broad face went white, and she stiffened as if the life had gone out of her. Only one thing could terrify Rebecca like that, Josiah knew—an Indian.

The cry came again, and it shattered the scene below like a rock against glass.

Jonathon let out his own cry and, flinging Elizabeth into the field, retreated down the path at a full gallop. He tore past Hope, grabbing Richard around the arm and half dragging him up the path. They disappeared into the mist as suddenly as they'd arrived.

Behind them, Hope sank to the ground and looked at the

sky as if the cry had come from there. In the underbrush, four heads popped up one by one, and Josiah could see the blank stares of shock on their faces.

Above them, Josiah squinted through the darkness and then blew the all-clear signal on his whistle. The merry band on the ground sprang from hiding and flung themselves on Hope in the path. They all nodded at once and then scattered, leaving only Hope shivering on the ground. They'd gone home, Josiah knew. Their work was done—and they were too scared to stay and celebrate.

Beside him, Rebecca shook like one of the last leaves on the trees.

"It's all right now, Rebecca," Josiah said to her.

He wasn't at all sure of that. An Indian had cried out, there was no doubt of that. But who was it? Where was he now? Were they still in danger?

Josiah had to pry Rebecca's arms from the tree, and it took a full five minutes to coax her down. On the ground she clung to him, still shaking, and he walked stiffly with her arms plastered around his leg.

"Josiah!" someone whispered.

Josiah jumped and then dragged Rebecca into the line of trees. Hope leaned behind one of them, tears trickling down her ashen face.

"The Putnams are gone," Josiah said. "I could see from the tree. I tried to warn you, Hope, but you couldn't hear—"

Hope waved him off. "Josiah, what was that—that noise, that scream?"

"Indian!" Rebecca's mouth flew open as if she could no

longer hold it closed, and it spewed out a tangle of words that made Josiah's head spin. "Indian!" she cried. "Bandits had Elizabeth! Indians were coming for them!" She flapped her hands up and down as if she could no longer stand the thoughts that collided with each other inside her head. "Elizabeth!" she cried over and over.

"Take her home," Josiah said.

Hope looked at him sharply. "Aren't you coming? Mama and Papa will be home soon."

"I'll be along."

"We've done it all—we've saved the wolves. Come home now, Josiah. What else is there to do?"

"I'll be along." Josiah tilted his chin at her and she sighed.

"I liked it better when you were a brainless boy," she muttered as she took Rebecca's hand. "At least you listened to me then."

Before they had rounded the bend, Josiah was off into the field. Jonathon had been right here when he'd flung Rebecca's doll and run away. Josiah didn't want to stay any more than Hope wanted him to, but it should only take a minute to find the doll. It might be the only thing that would stop Rebecca's hands from flapping.

He had to find it. He'd done too many bad things to Rebecca. He couldn't break this one promise to her.

Thomas Putnam's neglected cornfield looked bigger and darker than it had from the tree. The mist had become so thick, Josiah had to get down on his hands and knees and crawl if he was to have any hope of finding it. He pawed the ground, but the soil and dried husks went on forever.

I'll never find it, Josiah told himself. And for one crazy instant he almost called out, *Elizabeth, where are you?* He knew that's what Rebecca would have done.

"Boy!"

Josiah froze, and his fingers dug into the dirt. Had he heard that? It was more like the murmur of the wind—

"Boy!"

It came louder this time.

Josiah peered through the mist. Ahead of him, something blue appeared out of it.

"Wife of Wolf!" he whispered.

Her face creased into a map of pleased lines as she came toward him. She, too, was on her hands and knees, and something swung on a thin leather string from around her neck. Josiah blinked hard to focus on it. It certainly looked like—like one of his old whistles.

She stopped and held out her arm. Something soft touched Josiah's hand, and his fingers closed over Elizabeth. Everything else was chased out of his mind.

"Thank you," Josiah started to say, but footsteps behind them, crashing out of control through the dried husks, cut him off short.

"I hear you out here, Josiah Hutchinson! I know you're hiding—and we *will* get you!"

It was Jonathon.

"Help me!" Josiah whispered to the squaw. But she was gone. Josiah dug into the dirt and started to run.

And then from somewhere in the night came the terrifying scream again. Only this time, it sounded like angels singing to Josiah. The heavy footsteps behind him slid to a halt, and a cry of fear rose from Jonathon Putnam. The sound of his running feet quickly faded toward Thomas Putnam's farmhouse.

Josiah stayed crouched for a long time until he was sure Jonathon was panting by his uncle's fireplace. "Thank you, Wife of Wolf!" he whispered into the darkness.

For answer, he heard the timid tooting of a wooden whistle. He tucked Elizabeth under his arm and ran for home.

The Hutchinson house was dark and quiet except for the tiny fire Hope had left flickering and crackling in the kitchen. Josiah crept upstairs and peeked into Hope's bed. She was half sitting up against her bed cushions, rocking a fitful Rebecca in her arms.

"I found someone wandering in the woods!" Josiah said to his cousin.

He held out Elizabeth. Rebecca's arms flew out and wrapped themselves around the doll. Her soft, slack mouth covered Elizabeth with kisses until Josiah felt himself squirming. But Hope looked up at him, her eyes shiny with tears.

"You went back and got her? They could've found you, Josiah! You could be tied up in Thomas Putnam's kitchen right now!"

Josiah shrugged and ducked his head. "I'm going to bed now."

He turned to go, but a chubby, soggy little hand held onto his arm. "God bless you, Joshua," Rebecca said.

Then she turned over on Hope's bed and cradled the doll

against her. Her breathing was heavy and even within ten seconds. Hope gave a sigh and her eyes, too, drifted closed.

Josiah went to the window and sank heavily onto the trunk. "Thank you, God," he said.

Below him, he heard the clomping of oxen's hooves. His parents and Aunt Esther were coming up the road. In one smooth dive, Josiah was in his cot. And all was quiet in the Hutchinson house.

✢ ⋅✤⋅ ✢

on't drop this basket, Josiah, or I will drop *you* on your head."

Hope put a flat-bottomed Indian basket in his hand and kept her own hand on its handle as she looked into his eyes.

"Mince or pumpkin?" he said.

"Neither. Apple."

"I helped bake that one!"

Josiah turned at the voice that sounded like a baby foghorn and grinned at Rebecca. "Then I won't drop it," he said.

Mama, Aunt Esther, Hope, and even Rebecca had been baking for days. They kept him busy carrying in armload after armload of wood from the brisk November air into the steaming kitchen where they'd baked no less than 20 pies on cast-iron baking plates, removed them to wooden shingles, and placed them in baskets.

Josiah smiled now as he toted the apple pie in its basket. "Just perfect for carrying pies, Josiah!" Aunt Esther had exclaimed.

A few days after the wolf trap raid by the merry band, Josiah was crossing the Crane Bridge just below the sawmill, when Wife of Wolf had again whispered "Boy!" and appeared from out of nowhere. It was the first nose-biting cold day, and the blue shawl was wrapped tightly around her head and draped over her shoulders. Josiah had looked at once for the whistle around her neck but it was hidden. She'd held out her basket-laden arms and smiled and grunted.

"You want me to take one?" he'd said. "I have no money."

She shook her head and pushed the one at the end of her wrist toward him. It was big and flat-bottomed and just the right size for pies.

But Josiah hadn't taken it right away. She obviously understood English, even though she didn't speak it. Just like someone else he had known—

"Why do you protect me?" Josiah asked.

She pretended not to understand him, shaking her head and wrinkling her forehead.

"You're always there to help me," Josiah insisted. "Why?"

Still she shook her head, and for a moment Josiah thought she would turn and run. He pointed to the bright blue shawl now crossed over her chest—the one he had been so happy to see so many times these past few weeks.

"Why do you wear the white boy's whistle around your neck, then?" he said. "Where did you get it?"

Wife of Wolf straightened her shoulders and lifted her

chin, as if she had just been accused of stealing. Josiah was immediately sorry he'd said anything.

"Never mind—it's all right," Josiah said hurriedly. "Shall I take the basket?"

But Wife of Wolf stared at him with eyes that saw right through him. Slowly, she spoke. "Oneko."

Josiah stared, his outstretched hand suspended in the air between them. "Oneko? You got that whistle from Oneko?"

She nodded.

"But—I gave it to him—last spring."

She nodded again.

Josiah turned from her, just for a moment, to look down over the bridge into the water and collect his thoughts.

He turned back around to ask her a hundred questions— *How do you know Oneko? How is he? Does he still remember me? Can I see him again? Is his father still angry with me?* But she was gone. She'd slipped away as she always did. But she'd left the basket on the ground in front of him.

When he gave it to his mother as a present, she didn't even ask him where it came from.

Many questions went unasked these days. When the news started around the village that three of the Putnams' wolf traps had mysteriously been dismantled, Papa didn't ask them if they knew anything about it. And Joseph Putnam had never asked him if he and God got things figured out—he just looked at Josiah one day and said he thought perhaps they were getting close.

It was probably because so many other things were going on. There was the Thanksgiving feast at Joseph Putnam's house to prepare for. And the anxious waiting for news from Phillip English, who had gone to Boston to try to help Aunt Esther with Uncle Daniel's estate—he had even missed Joseph Putnam's wedding as a result. And the angry visits from the Putnams.

Three nights in a row one of the brothers clattered the heavy knocker on the Hutchinsons' front door and demanded to be let in. Each time Papa led the unwanted guest to the kitchen, for the nights were now snappish with the cold and to stand with the front door open meant the house would be almost misty as they huddled in their beds later. Once in the kitchen, every one of them—Thomas, John, and Nathaniel—accused Papa of ruining their wolf traps.

Papa just looked at Nathaniel, his bushy eyebrows almost touching the top of his forehead. "It's the first I've heard of such a thing, Nathaniel Putnam," Papa said. Even Nathaniel could see that he was telling the truth, and he stomped out muttering his disappointment.

When John Putnam came the next night, Papa was ready for him. "I wish I had thought of it, John," Papa told him, "but I can't take credit." He'd given a half smile then and said, "Are you getting enough rest, Putnam? You look somewhat—bewildered."

With each visit, Papa became more amused by their questions and pointing fingers, but Hope and Josiah sat rigidly in their seats and tried not to sweat. They always made sure Rebecca was shooed off to another room. She was sure to announce proudly that she had "helped."

But neither John nor Nathaniel mentioned a word about

the children who were seen—and almost caught—at Thomas Putnam's farm. When Thomas Putnam himself appeared on the third night, Josiah was sick to his stomach with fear. They hadn't lied to Papa to pull off the plan of action. He hoped they wouldn't have to tell him the truth now.

"You needn't waste your breath," Papa told Thomas that night in the kitchen before Mr. Putnam could even open his mouth. "I had nothing to do with the dismantling of your wolf trap—even though I find the practice of setting such traps cruel and inexcusable."

Thomas stood with his mouth agape for a second and scowled furiously. "I know it wasn't you, Hutchinson! Do you take me for a fool?"

"Aye," Hope muttered.

"Then, why are you here?" Papa said. "You must know you are not welcome in this house. Please state your business and be off with you."

"Sneaking around in the dead of night to damage another man's property is not your style, Hutchinson," Putnam said. "This has more of the Porters' mark upon it."

Papa's eyebrows nearly shot to his hairline. "Porters! Have you gone mad, man? The Porters were in Salem Town, as were you, the night you say this mischief took place."

"Mischief, you say? Joseph, I am trying to save my animals—perhaps even my family from these vicious wolves —"

Josiah jerked and Hope put a steadying hand on his knee.

"Now that my trap has been destroyed, I am open to attack."

Papa waved him off with an impatient hand. "If that is all

you have come here to whine about, Mr. Putnam, I beg you to take your leave. We have not even begun our Bible reading yet this evening, so if you would excuse us—"

"You'd best be reading your Bible and praying, Hutchinson. If you will not join the militia and help protect this village, you can at least ask for God's shield."

Papa sighed in annoyance. "Against what?"

"Indians."

"Ach!"

"There are Indians about!"

"Aye—selling baskets!"

"You yourself claim an Indian warning was pinned to your door."

Papa gave him a hard look.

"And what about the Indian war cries the other night!" Thomas Putnam blustered on.

Papa exploded into laughter.

"Laugh, then, Hutchinson, but am I to disbelieve my own son?"

Josiah caught his breath, and he felt Hope stiffen beside him.

"What does your son say?" Papa said, still chuckling to himself.

"On the very night my trap was removed, my son Richard and my nephew Jonathon heard an Indian war cry—not once, but twice, right on my farm—in my west field, Joseph Hutchinson!"

Papa's eyes shot to Josiah and Hope. Josiah knew he might as well confess right then, for he was certain the guilt was plastered from forehead to chin.

"You were both here that night—the night of Joseph Putnam's wedding," Papa said. "Did you hear any such war cries?"

We said we wouldn't lie, Josiah reminded himself. *It's time for the truth.*

But Hope gave him a gentle nudge in the side and cleared her throat. "*War* cries?"

"Aye," barked Thomas Putnam.

Hope looked at him straight on, her black eyes innocent. "I surely heard nothing that I know to be an Indian war cry—but then, I've never heard one before. Have Richard and Jonathon?"

At this Papa began to chuckle in earnest, and he even slapped Thomas Putnam good-naturedly on the back. "I think she has put some considerable doubt in your mind, eh, Thomas? How *would* your boys know an Indian war cry if they heard one? I don't think the village has ever heard the likes of any such thing." His face quickly darkened. "Now, as I asked you before, would you kindly take your leave?"

As Papa ushered Thomas Putnam to the door, Josiah breathed into Hope's ear, "I wonder why Jonathon and Richard didn't just tell that they saw us?"

Hope shook her head and shrugged.

It wasn't long before Josiah learned the answer. He was coming home from school, plodding along the road just above Nathaniel Putnam's house. The November wind was blowing so fiercely, he was surprised he heard Jonathon calling to him at all. His voice came to him thin and shrill from behind a barren tree at the edge of the property.

Josiah had almost broken into a run when he saw him, but something in the way Jonathon looked secretively over his shoulders as he hurried toward him slowed Josiah to a stop. He remembered feeling sorry for Jonathon once, for having a father like Nathaniel, and he felt like that again now. Jonathon looked lonely, like he had to find something to fill his time.

"I want to say something to you, Hutchinson," Jonathon said when he reached him. There was a good six feet of ground between them, enough room for Jonathon to pace nervously as he talked.

"Say it."

"We know."

Josiah waited. Jonathon stared hard at him, and Josiah finally realized he was supposed to be afraid.

But he wasn't. He wasn't afraid—because he had nothing left to *prove*. The thought made him smile.

"I see nothing funny," Jonathon said. "You think you've outsmarted us, and maybe you have this time. But there will be other times—and we will get you. We will get you then."

Josiah tried to make his eyes wide like Hope's when she was pretending to be innocent. "I'm sure I don't know what you're talking about."

Jonathon stopped pacing. "We know it was you who ruined the wolf traps. Your sister said she was out looking for her lost cow, but of course we never believed her for a minute."

Josiah choked back a laugh. He had never asked Hope

what story she'd used to get Jonathon and Richard to almost let her go. A lost cow wasn't bad for not having much warning.

"Are you laughing at me, Josiah Hutchinson?" Jonathon said angrily.

"No!" Josiah said quickly. "I was just wondering. Why did you not tell your father and your uncles that you saw us there?"

Jonathon took a step toward him, but Josiah didn't step back. Jonathon took another step, so that the tips of their noses nearly touched. "If I told them about that—or about your little friendship with the Indian squaw," he said tightly through his teeth, "then we would not have the pleasure of getting you and your little army ourselves. Let the adults have their war. We have ours now. And I warn you, Hutchinson—we will win."

He turned crisply on his heel and marched away. Behind him, Josiah Hutchinson stood laughing silently.

"If you are going to stand there smiling to yourself," Papa said at Josiah's elbow now, "we shall never get to Joseph Putnam's—and all the tarts will be eaten without us."

"And the wild turkey!" Rebecca chimed in, loudly, of course, "and the cheese and the nuts and the pies—"

"We have the pies here," Josiah told her.

"—and we shall miss the games and the fiddlers—"

Papa shook his head. "Don't tell her anything you don't want her to remember."

Rebecca's description of Thanksgiving at Joseph Putnam's new house was not far wrong. Long tables scored the best room, and they were piled with every kind of treat Rebecca had named and then some. She followed Hope importantly into the kitchen to deliver a pie, while Josiah stood, open-mouthed, eyeing the feast they were about to enjoy. Few parties and celebrations were allowed in Puritan society, so each one was savored and dreamed of and drooled over for weeks.

But Josiah's eyes were torn from the tables as the men's voices drifted in from Joseph Putnam's study next door. Above his father's solid tones and Joseph's merry ones and the important barks of the Porters, he heard another familiar voice that made him break into a smile. Phillip English was here from Salem Town. At the table he would tell stories about the ships, the *Adventure* and the *Hutchinson*. Josiah never grew tired of hearing about the sea.

Moments later, when they gathered around the tables, Rebecca slipped into a seat beside Josiah and looked up at him. "I am sitting next to you, Joshua."

"Aye," Josiah said. And he smiled at her.

From across the table, a worn hand reached over and touched his. Josiah looked up in surprise at Aunt Esther whose pale, tired eyes looked right into his.

"No one has ever been quite so kind to my daughter," she said. "If we ever do leave here, I know she will never forget you. I am grateful."

Josiah wasn't sure what to say. He mumbled, "Aye—thank you," and he felt the red filling up his cheeks. *He* was grateful when Phillip English stood up and tapped his elegant walking stick against his chair.

"Our host will, of course, offer the prayers of Thanksgiving at this first feast in his home," Phillip said in his smooth, educated voice. "But I would like to announce something that I think we will all want to give thanks for today."

A ripple ran through the tables.

"I have been to Boston," Phillip English went on, "and I am pleased to say that I was able to reach a settlement for Goody Esther concerning her estate." He turned kindly to Aunt Esther. "You are now free to claim Daniel Hawkes's estate in Hingham if you wish. And I would like to offer to see that you and your daughter reach there safely before the winter sets in."

A happy shriek went up along the tables. Mama rose from her seat to hug Aunt Esther, and Papa beamed as Josiah had not seen him do in many months. Across the table, Hope clapped and danced in her seat. Beside him came a tug at his sleeve.

"Why is Mama crying?" Rebecca shouted above the noise.

Josiah wasn't sure, but he took a guess. "I think she's happy."

"Why?"

"Because you can go home to Hingham now."

The celebration shimmer left Rebecca's face. "Are you coming with us, Joshua?"

For some reason, the answer stuck in Josiah's throat. He could only shake his head.

Slowly, Rebecca began to shake hers. "Then, I can't go," she said. "I will stay here with you."

Josiah looked helplessly at Hope, but she couldn't hear through the clatter of happy voices around them. Rebecca tugged again at his shirt.

"Why can't you come with us?" she asked.

"Because Papa needs me here, and Mama, too. The children—the children have to help their parents. The times are changing now, and they need us."

Rebecca's face puckered as she tried to understand, but still she shook her head.

Josiah moved Elizabeth from Rebecca's arms to the table and took his cousin's two chunky hands in his. "Since you've been here, you've helped us, eh?" he said.

Rebecca bobbed her head up and down until her cap bounced off.

"Aye—and now, Rebecca, it's time for you to help your mama. You must go with her and help her. The parents need the children now."

Josiah held his breath and watched the wheels inside Rebecca's head turning. They were grinding slowly, but they were turning. She looked at her mother and then back at Josiah and once again at Aunt Esther. Finally, she stopped and looked into Josiah's eyes. His heart thudded. For that brief instant, her big, pale eyes were full of wisdom, a wisdom that told Josiah that imitating animals was not Rebecca's only gift.

"Let us bow our heads in prayer," Joseph Putnam said softly.

Josiah pulled his hands away and put them in his lap with fingers entwined. He closed his eyes, and as Joseph Putnam began to pray, he felt something soft pass across his lap and rest on his knees. He opened his eyes, and there was

Elizabeth sprawled across his legs.

"She wants to stay here with you while I go to Hingham," Rebecca whispered hoarsely. "You are her papa now—and the children need their parents."

Joseph Putnam prayed on, and Rebecca put her chubby hands in her lap and closed her eyes. Josiah closed his again, too. And he felt one of his own warm tears splash onto his fingers.

✢ ✢ ✢

ut my cloak around you, Josiah. You're shivering."
Joseph Hutchinson reached behind his seat on the
wagon and pulled out a long, brown woolen cloak
that he handed to his son.

Josiah wrapped it around him and looked miserably out at
the gray November evening. He felt his father looking down
at him, but he didn't look back.

"You are somewhat saddened, Josiah," Papa said finally.

Josiah nodded.

"And I have made it worse by leaving Salem Town tonight,
instead of waiting and seeing them off on Phillip English's
ship tomorrow."

It was more a statement than a question, but it was a true
one, and once again Josiah nodded.

The oxen plodded on up the Ipswich Road, drawing closer
to Salem Village. Josiah glared at the bare trees. He felt as

empty as they looked, and he wasn't sure why. It was only his cousin who had left, after all, and a girl at that—one who asked "Why?" almost more than she blinked or breathed.

But her going was leaving him stripped somehow—just like losing someone always did. And he'd lost so many lately. First the Widow Hooker. Then Oneko. Now Rebecca. Aye—he *was* as gray and lonely as one of those trees. He was sure he wouldn't feel this bad if he could have only led Rebecca up the gangplank and answered her questions about the ship she'd be sailing on to Hingham so she wouldn't be afraid—

"You seem to have developed quite an imagination, Josiah," his father said suddenly. "You seem to have no trouble devising clever schemes and such."

Josiah looked at him quickly, and his heart immediately began to thump in his ears.

"Is that not true?" Papa said.

"Aye, sir."

"Good. Then, let you use your imagination now. I want you to picture yourself tomorrow morning, standing on Phillip English's dock, watching Rebecca's ship go out to sea. Can you do that?"

The picture came instantly to Josiah's mind and he nodded, but his thoughts were racing. What was Papa talking about?

"Imagine, too, your cousin, leanin' against the railing as the anchor is hoisted and the ship begins to leave the wharf. What is she doing, Josiah?"

The picture was clear in Josiah's mind. He didn't even have to squint.

"What is she doing?" Papa asked again.

"She—she's—she's crying."

"Of course she is. For some reason that child fastened herself to you like tallow to a candlewick, and to find herself torn away from you—well, I imagine she'd be doing more than crying, son. I imagine your Aunt Esther would be hard put to find a way to calm her before they even got to Boston. Do you get my meaning?"

Josiah did. The last time he'd seen Rebecca she was sleeping on the same big bed Josiah had slept in last summer with her arm curled around a doll made of silk with a painted face that Mary English had tucked in beside her. She wouldn't see it until morning.

On their arrival at the English house, Rebecca had seen little Judith English lugging a doll around and had told Mrs. English with solemn eyes, "I don't have a doll. I left Elizabeth with Josiah. He's her papa now."

Josiah had wanted to dig a hole through the floor and dive in. As it was he escaped to the kitchen to beg for macaroons. The next thing he knew, Rebecca danced in to say good night—and neither of them had known it would be their last good-bye.

After she went upstairs, Papa told him they'd be leaving in a few minutes for home, and Josiah dashed up to her room, but she was already sound asleep.

He hadn't kissed her or anything. She'd done enough slobbering on his cheeks ever since she found out she was leaving. But he had crept up to the bed and whispered in her ear, "Don't be afraid, Rebecca. If you need anything, just remember to run straight to God. I'll probably be doing that, too. Y'see, there are some things I never told you—about the lies I said to scare you. I think I explained all those things. I just wanted you to know I—I'm sorry."

Papa was right. Rebecca slept peacefully on. No tears—from her or from him.

"Aye, sir," Josiah said now. "I get your meaning."

His father nodded and was quiet.

But Josiah didn't feel any better. It was cold, and the winter stretched ahead. The golden days of autumn were over, and everything had changed—just as it always seemed to do.

Papa turned the wagon off the Ipswich Road and headed toward the Hutchinson farm. They were almost home, and Josiah was eager to be in his cot alone. But Papa slowed the oxen and reached out his hand.

"Do you feel that, Josiah?" he said.

Josiah shook his head, but he stuck out his hand, palm up. Into it fell tiny, sparkling flakes of snow.

"First of the winter," Papa said softly, and then he sighed. "I wonder what this winter shall bring, eh?" He sat up straight to continue on, but then Josiah saw his forehead wrinkle. "What's this now?"

From down the road, Josiah heard the clomping of a horse's hooves. He leaned out the side of the wagon and peered through the snow that was falling harder now. A thin man rode his horse slowly toward them, as if he were in no hurry at all—as if he had a great deal to think about on the way.

"'Tis Reverend Parris." Papa's eyes flickered, and Josiah knew he was ready to do battle if he needed to.

He pulled the wagon to the side, but Reverend Parris passed without a word to the Hutchinsons. His collar was pulled up around his neck, and his hat almost covered his face. They knew who he was only by the hunch of his shoulders as he clumped by.

Papa shook his head, and Josiah saw the sparks go out of his eyes.

"I believe there is some good in the man," Papa muttered. "I pray we can heal this wound in his church somehow." Then softly, he urged the oxen on.

Josiah had once decided that Papa was like fire. He could flare up when he needed to, but as soon as the need passed, the flames were put out and he just flickered slowly on.

At the time he'd thought that, Josiah remembered, he didn't know what he himself was like. Now he cocked his head and turned to watch the minister disappear behind them. He was a lonely figure, etched against the sky in his black cloak with the snow dusting his head and back.

What is it like in his house? Josiah thought. *Do they gather around the fire and pop corn? Is there anyone there who knows why he's sad, the way Papa does me?*

Josiah shivered, even in his father's heavy cloak. The only thing missing from the picture of the Reverend Samuel Parris vanishing into the snow was the howling of a wolf. But the wolves were quiet tonight. *They must have no reason to speak, Josiah thought. They've already* proven *themselves.*

Josiah turned to look up at his fiery father whose fire was now crackling pleasantly. The lines in his face were smooth, and his big, comfortable shoulders rocked with the swaying of the wagon as he looked out at the snow.

Papa was like fire. Was he, Josiah, like the wolves? Sometimes he was lonely—like Reverend Parris and Hope and Rebecca, and even Jonathon Putnam. Sometimes, as Joseph Putnam put it, he was misunderstood, even by himself. He would fight for the people he loved if he was cornered. And he was silent when there was no need to be anything else.

Josiah nodded to himself. He had never told anyone about the wolf he'd met that day he was tied up in the Putnams' trap. He didn't want to have to *prove* it to anyone, for one thing. And it seemed like a secret that should be kept between him and the wolf. But he had started to believe something that day, and he hadn't even known it until now. He *was* like the wolves. He'd *proven* himself this fall. There was no need to *prove* anything anymore. He'd figured it out—no, he and God had figured it out.

Like his father, Josiah looked at the snow. It was a new season now. The seasons always changed, just like everything did. But what *would* this new season bring? More adventures? Another new person into his life, as this one had brought Rebecca and Wife of Wolf? Would it tell him who this Indian squaw was—and how she'd come to wear the whistle he had given Oneko?

Suddenly, Josiah yawned and pulled his father's big, comforting cloak tighter around him. He wouldn't think about that now. Right now he would think about the fire waiting in the Hutchinson kitchen—

"Do you imagine there is some corn for popping at home?" Papa said.

Josiah looked at him quickly and grinned. Aye, he imagined there was—because like the wolves, Josiah Hutchinson could imagine the most wonderful schemes.

✢ ✢ ✢

1. Lt. John Putnam
2. Widow's Cabin
3. Joseph Putnam
4. Sgt. Putnam
5. Capt. Walcott
6. Rev. Parris
7. Meeting House
8. Nathan Ingersoll
9. Nathaniel Putnam
10. Israel Porter
11. Dr. Griggs
12. John Porter's Mill
13. John & Elizabeth Proctor

A Map of
SALEM VILLAGE
& Vicinity in 1692

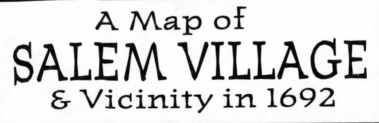

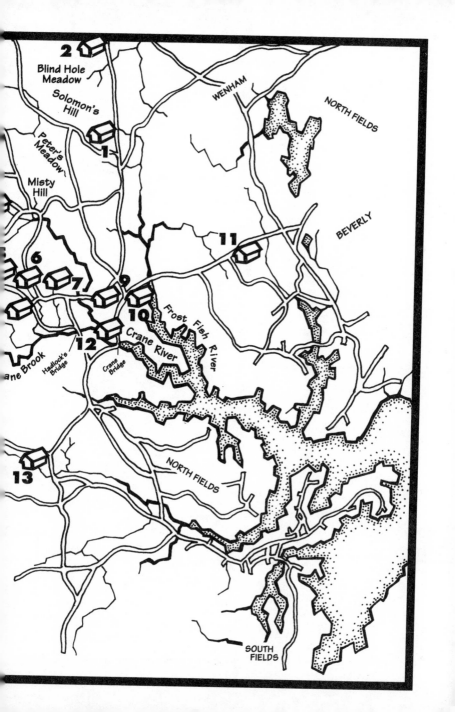

There's More Adventure in the Christian Heritage Series!

The Rescue #1

Josiah had wished there was no Hope in his life! But that was before the accident, when he and his older sister, Hope, fought a lot. Now, she's very sick. And neither the town doctor nor all the family's wishing can save her. Their only earthly chance is an old widow—a stranger to Salem Village—whose very presence could destroy the family's relationship with everyone else! Can she save Hope? And at what price?

The Stowaway #2

Josiah is going to town! Sent to Salem Town to be educated, Josiah Hutchinson's dream of someday becoming a sailor now seems within reach, and nothing is going to stop him . . . or so he thinks! A tough orphan named Simon has other plans, and his evil schemes could get both Josiah and Hope in a heap of trouble. How will the kids prove their innocence? Who's story will the village believe?

Available at a fine Christian bookstore near you.

Focus on the Family Publications

Focus on the Family

    This complimentary magazine provides inspiring stories, thought-provoking articles and helpful information for families interested in traditional, biblical values. Each issue also includes a "Focus on the Family" radio broadcast schedule.

Brio

    Designed especially for teen girls, *Brio* is packed with super stories, intriguing interviews and amusing articles on the topics they care about most—relationships, fitness, fashion and more—all from a Christian perspective.

Breakaway

    With colorful graphics, hot topics and humor, this magazine for teen guys helps them keep their faith on course and gives the latest info on sports, music, celebrities . . . even girls. Best of all, this publication shows teens how they can put their Christian faith into practice and resist peer pressure.

All magazines are published monthly except where otherwise noted. For more information regarding these and other resources, please call Focus on the Family at (719) 531-5181, or write to us at Focus on the Family, Colorado Springs, CO 80995.